CW00858031

1 MONTH OF
FREE
READING

at

www.ForgottenBooks.com

By purchasing this book you are eligible for one month membership to ForgottenBooks.com, giving you unlimited access to our entire collection of over 1,000,000 titles via our web site and mobile apps.

To claim your free month visit:

www.forgottenbooks.com/free433331

ISBN 978-0-266-36291-3
PIBN 10433331

THE WORKS OF
DONALD G. MITCHELL

WITH BASEMENT
AND ATTIC

CHARLES SCRIBNER'S SONS
NEW YORK ✹ ✹ ✹ ✹ 1907

DEDICATORY LETTER

TO DR. FORDYCE BARKER

My Dear Doctor:

This book of Seven Stories, before which I inscribe your name, is made up from thofe fpecial reminifcences of travel, which—after a lapfe of ten years—hang strongeft in my mind. I think there are fome paffably good things in it; and fome, I fear, which are not fo good. Thus far, it is unlike your practice, of which the foundness is uniform.

At beft, I count the book only a little bundle of fagots which I have fet to crackle away under the kettle, where I hope fome day to cook a more favory mefs. And though there be not much in this which fhall ftick to the ribs, I hope there is nothing that will breed in any man an indigestion. I think you count light food fometimes a good dietary; and unlefs I am mistaken, I have known you, on occasions, to fmother a pill in a fyllabub. And if I have tried to drop here and there, in the courfe of thefe pages, a nugget of wholefome fentiment, I hope it may prove as good a tonic as any of your iodides.

I feel reafonably certain that the charge for

it will be fmaller:—but on this fcore, I cannot fpeak pofitively, fince your generofity always keeps me your debtor.

Very truly your friend,

DONALD G. MITCHELL.

EDGEWOOD, April, 1864.

CONTENTS

vii

CONTENTS

ILLUSTRATIONS

BASEMENT

SERVING FOR INTRODUCTION

BASEMENT

I N an out of the way corner of my library are five plethoric little note-books of Travel. One of them, and it is the earliest, is bound in smart red leather, and has altogether a dapper British air; its paper is firm and evenly lined, and it came a great many years ago (I will not say how many) out of a stationer's shop upon Lord street in Liverpool. A second, in stiff boards, marbled, and backed with muslin, wears a soldierly primness in its aspect that always calls to mind the bugles, and the drums, and the brazen helmets of Berlin —where, once upon a time, I added it to my little stock of travelling companions. A third, in limp morocco, bought under the Hotel *de l'Ecu* at Geneva, shows a great deal of the Swiss affectation of British wares, and has borne bravely the hard knapsack service, and the many stains which belonged to those glorious mountain tramps that live again whenever I turn over its comely pages. Another is

3

tattered, dingy—the paper frail, and a half of its cover gone; yet I think it is a fair specimen of what the Roman stationers could do, in the days when the Sixteenth Gregory was Pope. The fifth and last, is coquettish, jaunty—as prim as the Prussian, limp like the Genevese, and only less solid than the English: it is all over French; and the fellows to it may very likely have served a tidy *grisette* to write down her tale of finery, or some learned member of the Institute to record his note-takings in the Imperial Library.

I dare not say how often these little conjurers of books wean me away from all graver employment, and tempt me to some ramble among the highlands of Scotland, or the fastnesses of the Apennines. I do not know but that this refreshment of the old sentiment of travel, through the first unstudied jottings-down, is oftentimes more delightful than a repeated visit.

To-night—by a word, by a fragment of a line, dropped upon my little Genevese book, the peak of Mont Blanc cleaves the sky for the first time in all my range of vision; the clear, up-lifted mountain of white, just touched with the rosy hues of approaching twilight—the blue brothers of nearer mountains shouldering up the monarch—the dark, low fir forests fringing all the valley up which I look—a shining streak of road that beckons me on to the Chamouni worship—the river (is it the Arve?) glistening and roaring a great song—all this my little book summons, freshly, and without disturbing object. But if I repeat the visit, the inevitable comparisons present themselves. "Aye, this is it; but the atmosphere is not altogether so clear, or the approach is not so favorable;" and so, for mere vanity's sake, you must give a fellow-passenger the benefit of your previous knowledge: as if all the *"le voici!"* and *"le voilà!"* were not the merest impertinences in such august presence! No: it is sadly true—perhaps pleasantly true—that there are scenes of which no second sight will enlarge the bounds wherein imagination may disport itself,—for which no second sight will create an atmosphere of more glorious rarity.

To-night, this tattered little Roman journal, by merest mention of the greasy, cushioned curtain, under whose corner I first urged my way into the great aisle of St. Peter's—brings up the awed step with which I sidled down the marble pavement, breathing that soft atmosphere, perfumed with fading incense—oppressed, as by a charm, with the thought of that genius which had conjured this miracle of architecture; and oppressed (I know not how) by a thought of that Papal hierarchy which by such silent show of pomp and power, had compelled the service of millions. And if I go back again, all this delightfully vague estimate of its grandeur cannot renew itself; the height is the same; all the width is there; those cherubs who hold the font are indeed giants; but the aroma of first impressions is lost in a whirl of new comparisons and estimates; is the Baldachino indeed as high as they say it is? Is St. Peter's toe, of a truth worn away with the inveterate kissings? Every piece of statuary, every glowing blazon of mosaic compels an admeasurement of the old fancy with the object itself. All the charming, intoxicating generality of impression is preyed upon, and absorbed piecemeal by specialities of inference, or of observation; while here, in the quiet of my room, with no distracting object in view, I blunder through the disorderly characters of my notebook with all the old glow upon me, and start to life again that first, rich, Roman dream.

And the same is true of all lesser things: There was once a peasant girl, somewhere in

INTRODUCTION

Normandy, with deliciously quaint muslin head-dress, and cheeks like the apricots she sold,—a voice that rippled like a song; and yet, with only a half line of my blotted note-book, she springs into all that winsome, co-quettish life which sparkled then and there in her little Norman town; but if I were to leave the pleasant cheatery of my book, and travel never so widely, all up and down through Normandy, I could never meet with such a blithe young peasant again.

By one or two of the old pen-marks, I am reminded of a burly beggar, encountered in my first stroll through Liverpool. He was without any lower limbs that I could discover, and was squatted upon the stone flagging of St. Nicholas' church-yard, where he asked charity with the authoritative air of a commander of an army. And I recall with a blush the admiring spirit with which, as a fresh and timid traveller, I yielded my pence to his impetuous summation; and how I reckoned his masterful manner fairly typical of the sturdy British empire, which squatted upon its little islands of the sea, demanded—in virtue only of its big head and shoulders—tribute of all the world. I do not believe that such imaginative exaltation of feeling could overcome me upon

a repeated visit; or if it did, that it would be-
get—as then—the very romanticism of charity.

There was a first-walk—scored down in the
red-covered book—along a brook-side in the
forest near to Blair-Athol in the north of Scotland,—in the course of which all the songs of
Burns that I had ever known, or heard, came
soughing to my ear through the fir-branches,
as if ploughmen in plaids had sung them; but
if I should go there again, I think the visionary ploughmen would sing no more; and that
I should be estimating the growth of the
larches, or wondering if the trout would rise
briskly to a hackle?

I do not write thus, simply to iterate the stale
truism, that the delight and freshness of first
impressions of travel, can never be renewed;
that we all know; all enthusiasms have but one
life, in the same mind. Convictions may be renewed, and gain strength and consistency by
renewal; but those enthusiasms which find their
life in exultant imaginative foray, can no more
be twice entertained, than a foaming beaker
of Mumm's Imperial can be twice drank.

What I wish to claim for my spotty note-
books, is—that their cabalistic signs revive
more surely and freshly the aroma of first im-

pressions than any renewed visit could do. Therefore I cherish them. Time and time again, I take them down from their niche in my library, when no more serious work is in hand, and glide insensibly into their memories, —the present slipping from me like a dream,— and indulge in that delightful bewilderment at which I have hinted, and in which cities and mountains pile before me, as if I lived among them.

It is true that the loose and disjointed wording in which I have scored down incidents or scenes of travel, would prove wholly uninteresting, if not absolutely unintelligible, to others. There are little catch-words, by the sight of which I may set a great river aflow, or build a temple; there are others, that start a company of dead faces from their graves, or put me in the middle of a great whirl of masked figures who dance the night out to the music of Musard. And I must say that I rather enjoy this symbolism of language, which individuates a man's private memories. Who knows what cold, invidious eye may be scanning them some day?

Let me satisfy the reader's curiosity—if I have succeeded in arousing any—by a little sample. It is taken from my dapper-looking

British note-book, and is dated "London, ——" (near twenty years ago), and runs thus:—"Arrival—night time—sea of lights—order—clattering cab—immense distances—whither going?—Covent Garden—no money—wanderings—American Prof.—tight cloak—Cornhill—Post-office—anxieties—relief."

Can the reader make anything of it? If he cannot, I think that I can and will. It brings to mind the first approach to London, and all the eager wonder with which I came bowling down upon it at dusk: this side and that, I look for tokens of the great Babylon; but the air is murky and dim, and it is past sunset; still I look, peering through the gloom. At last, there can be no mistake; a wilderness of lamps, far as I can see—east and west—fret the horizon with a golden line. On and on we hurtle over the rail, and always—east and west—the golden lamp-line of horizon stretches until we are fairly encircled by it, and the murky atmosphere has changed into a yellow canopy of smoke, under which—of a sudden—we halt, in London.

There is order; I remember that. There is somewhere a particular cab in a great line of cabs, of which I become presently the occupant, in virtue of the system which seems to govern passengers, railways, stations, cabmen and all. There is a wilderness of streets,—of shining shop-fronts,—of silent, tall houses, —of brother cabs, rattling our way—rattling the contrary way; there is a flicker of lanterns on a river, where steamers with checkered pipes go by like ghosts; there is a plunge into narrow streets, and presently out we go into broad and dazzling ones; on and on, we pass, by shops that show butchers' stores, shops that are party-colored with London haberdashery, drug shops, shops with bonnets, shops with books, shops with bakers' wares; a long, bright clattering drive, it seems to me, before I am landed in Covent Garden square.

Yet—how well I remember—under all the boyish excitement of a first visit, there lay a covert embarrassment and anxiety; for by the most awkward of haps, I chanced upon that first night in London, to be nearly penniless. It is rather a sorry position to be in, at almost any time; but for a young stranger, whose excitable brain is half addled by the throng of novelties and of splendor, in the largest city of the world, and whose nearest familiar friends are three thousand miles away—the money-less condition is awkward indeed. I had even cruel apprehensions that I should not be able to meet the demands of the cabman; in these, however, I was fortunately mistaken; and with six half-pence in my pocket I found myself for the first time a guest at a London inn.

I had, indeed, ordered remittances to be sent me there, from the Continent; but in due course of mail the reply could not arrive till next day. And who could tell what might happen to the mail? If I had only placed a little curb upon my curiosity in the southern counties, and not loitered as I did about Salisbury, and Stonehenge, and Winchester!

I awoke upon a murky morning in full sight of Covent Garden market; and could I believe my eyes?—were strawberries on sale under this chilling March gloom? I rang the bell, and sent my card below, with an inquiry for letters.

No letters had come.

I ate my breakfast nervously—though the chops were done to a turn, and the muffins were even less leathern than usual. I spent the greater part of the day sauntering between Charing Cross, Temple Bar, and the River. I have no dislike to a good, wearisome walk; most people, with only six half-pence in their pockets, have not.

I kept my room during the evening (although Jenny Lind was figuring in the *Son-*

nambula on the next block) and in the morning, after mail-time, sent the servant down again with my card—for letters.

He returned very promptly, with the reply, —"No letters this morning, Sir."

"Ah!" (And I think I crowded as much of hypocrisy into the expression, as ever man did.)

The chops on this morning were even better than yesterday; and the muffins were positively light;—I could have sworn they had been baked within the hour.

As I sat ruminating over the grate, the thought struck me that I had possibly made an error in the address left with the Paris banker. I can hardly tell why, but there seemed to me a sudden confusion in my mind between the names of Covent Garden and Cornhill. Possibly I had ordered my letters addressed to Cornhill? I had, unfortunately, no memoranda to guide me: to one of these two localities I was sure that I had requested remittances to be directed. What if they were lying at No. 9 Cornhill?

Everybody who has been in London knows that a crowded and weary walk lies between the two places; but there were no pennies to be spared for the omnibus people, however cajolingly they might beckon. So I entered bravely upon the tramp: and who should I come upon half down Fleet street, under the shadow of St. Bride's, but my old Latin professor, whom I had seen last in the plank box that forms the dais in the recitation room of a quiet New England college. If Ergasilus (of the *Capteivi*—whose humor the old gentleman dearly loved) had stepped out of a haberdasher's shop, and confronted me with talk about his chances of a prospective dinner, I could hardly have been more surprised.

His white hair, his stooping figure, his cloak gathered tightly about him, his keen eye, fairly dancing with boyish excitement—all these formed a picture I can never forget. We passed a pleasant word or two of salutation, and of as quick adieux; only words—*"verbæ sine penu et pecuniâ"*—(and the old gentleman's alliterative rendering of it came back to me as I stood there penniless).

After parting, I turned to watch him, as he threaded his way along the Fleet street walk; —quick, nervous, glancing everywhere; if only our sleepy college cloisters could get a more frequent airing!

In an hour and a half thereafter, I found myself, utterly fagged, pacing up and down the sidewalk of Cornhill. I found a Number Nine. I made appeal after my missing letter at a huckster's shop on the street.

They knew nothing of it.

I next made application in a dark court of the rear.

"There was niver a gintleman of that name lived here."

I asked, in my innocence,—"if the postman were in possession of such a letter, would he leave it?"

"Not being a boording-house—in coorse not."

My next aim was to intercept the Cornhill postman himself. Fortunately, the British postmen are all designated by red cuffs and collars; I made an eager rush at some three or four, whom I espied in the course of an hour or more of watch. They were all bound to other parts of the city

By this time I had an annoying sense of being constantly under the eye of a tall policeman in the neighborhood. I thought I observed him pointing me out with an air of apprehension, to a comrade, whose beat joined his upon the corner of the next street.

I had often heard of the willingness to communicate information on the part of the London police, and determined to divert the man's suspicions (if he entertained any) by explaining my position. I thought he listened incredulously. However, he assured me very positively, that if I should see the Cornhill postman on his beat (which I might not for three hours to come), he would deliver to me no letter, unless at the door to which it might be addressed, and then only unless I was an acknowledged inmate.

He advised me to make inquiries at the General Post-office

Under his directions, I walked, wearily, to the General Post-office. One may form some idea of the General Post-office of London by imagining three or four of our Fifth Avenue reservoirs placed side by side, flanked with Ionic columns, topped with attics, and pierced through by an immense hall, on either side of which are doors and traps innumerable.

I entered this hall, in which hundreds were moving about like bees—one to this door, and one to another—and all of them with a most enviable rapidity and precision of movement (myself, apparently, being the only lost or doubtful one), and read, with a vain bewilderment, the numerous notices of "Ship for India"—"Mails here close at 3.15"—"Packages over a pound at the next window, left"—"All newspapers mailed at this window must be in wrappers"—"Charge on Sydney letters raised twopence"—"Bombay mail closes at two, this day"—"Stamps only."

Fluttering about for a while, in a sad state of trepidation, I made a bold push for an open window, where an active gentleman had just mailed six letters for Bombay, and began—"Please, Sir, can you tell me about the Cornhill postman?"

"Know nothing about him!" and slap went the window.

I next made an advance to the newspaper trap—rapped—open flew the door: "I wish to inquire," said I, "about a letter—"

"Next window to left!" and click went the trap.

I marched with some assurance to the window on the left: the same pantomime was gone through. "I want to know," I began, more boldly, "about a letter directed to Cornhill."

"Know nothing about it, Sir; this is n't the place, you know."

"And pray where is the place, if you please?" (This seemed a very kindly man.)

"Oh, dear!—well,—I should say,—now, the

place was—let me see—over the **way** somewhere. It 's City, you know."

I thanked him; indeed I had no time **to** do
more, for the window was closed.

I marched over the way—that is, to the opposite side of the hall. I rapped at a new
trap: click! it flew open. "I wish to inquire,"
said I, "about a letter which the Cornhill postman may have taken by accident—"

"Oh—*may* have taken: better find out if he
really *did,* you know; for if he *did n't,* you see,
it 's no use, you know, t' inquire." And—
click!—the trap closed.

How to find out now if he really did? If
I could only see the Cornhill postman, who,
from the nature of his trust, could hardly be
very officious, I might hope at least for some
information. My eyes fell at this juncture
upon a well-fed porter, in royal livery, who was
loitering about the great entrance-gates of
the establishment, and seemed to be a kind of
civic beadle.

I ventured an appeal to him about the probable whereabouts of the Cornhill postmaı

"Oh, Corn'ill postm'n; dear me! I should
say, now, p'r'aps he *might* be down to the pay-
office. That 's to the right, out o' the yard,
down a halley—second flight o' 'igh steps,
like."

I went out of the yard, and down the alley, and applied, as directed, at the second flight of steps. Right for once; it *was* the pay-office.

"Was the Cornhill postman there?"

"He was not."

"Where would I probably find him?"

"He was paid off, with the rest, every Saturday morning at nine o'clock—precisely."

It was now Tuesday: I had allowed myself on this occasion, only a week for London. My anticipations of an enjoyable visit were not high.

I returned once more to the communicative porter. I think I touched my hat in preface of my second application (you will remember that I was fresh from the Continent): "You see," said he, "they goes to the 'stributing office, and all about, and it 's 'ard to say ajust where he might be; might be to Corn'ill—*poss'bly;* might *not* be, you know; might be 'twixt here and there; 'stributing office is to the left—third court, first flight, door to right."

I made my way to the distributing office; it seemed a "likely place" to find the man I was in search of. I found the door described by my stout friend, the porter, and entered very boldly. It opened upon an immense hall, resembling a huge church, with three tiers of galleries running around the walls, along which I saw scores of postmen, passing and repassing, in what seemed interminable confusion. I had scarce crossed the threshold when I was encountered by an official of some sort, who very brusquely demanded my business. I explained that I was in search of the Cornhill postman.

"This is no place to seek him, Sir; he comes here for his letters, and is off directly. No strangers are allowed here, Sir."

The man seemed civil, though peremptory.

"For Heaven's sake," said I, appealingly, "can you tell me how, or where, I *can* see the man who distributes the Cornhill letters?"

"I really can't, Sir."

"Could you tell me possibly where the man lives?"

"Really could n't, Sir; don't know at all; de'say it would n't be far."

I think he saw my look of despair, for he continued in a kinder tone: "Dear me, eh— did you, p'raps, eh—might I ask, eh—what your business might be with the, eh—Cornhill postman?"

I caught at what seemed my last hope. "I wanted," said I, "to make an inquiry—"

He interrupted—"Oh, dear me—bless me
—an inquiry! Why, you see, there 's an office for *inquiry*. It 's here about—round the
corner; you 'll see the window as you turn;
closes at three (looking at his watch); you 've,
eh—six minutes, just."

I went around the corner; I found the window.—"Office for Inquiry," posted above.
There was a man who stuttered, asking about
a letter which he had mailed for Calcutta two
months before, to the address of "Mr. T-t-t-th-
thet-Theodore T-t-tr-tret-Trenham."

I never heard a stutterer with less charity
before. A clock was to be seen over the head
of the office clerk within. I watched it with
nervous anxiety. The Calcutta applicant at
length made an end of his story. The clerk
turned to the clock. Two minutes were allowed me.

I had arranged a short story. The clerk
took my name, residence, address—promised
that the matter should be looked after.

I walked back to Covent Garden, weary,
but satisfied.

The next morning the waiter handed me
a letter addressed properly enough, "——
——, No. 9 Covent Garden."

The banker's letter had been delayed. My

search through the London office had been entirely unnecessary.

Three days after, and when I was engrossed with Madame Tussaud's wax-work and the Vauxhall wonders, and had forgotten my trials of Cornhill, I received a huge envelope, under the seal of the General Post-office of London, informing me that no letter bearing my address had been distributed to the Cornhill carrier during the last seven days; and advising me that, should such an one be received at the London Post-office, it would, in obedience to my wishes, be promptly delivered at No. 9 Covent Garden Square.

For aught I know, the officials of the London office may be looking for that letter still.

I hope not.

Shall I detach another memory from this mosaic of note books?

It is the figure of a ship that I see, making her way slowly, and lumberingly out of the Havre docks. The little jetty where the old round tower stood (they tell me it is gone now) is crowded with people; for it is a day of *fête*, and the idlers have nothing better to occupy them for the hour, than to watch the trim American vessel as she hauls out into the stream. As we slip through the dock gates there is a chorus of voices from the quay— "Adieu!" *"Bon voyage!"* and the emigrants who crowd the deck shout and wave a reply. A bearded man meantime, is counting and seoring them off, and ordering them below. There are crates of cabbages, huge baskets of meats, red-shirted sailors; and I hear from some quarter the cackle of poultry, and see a cow's head peering inquiringly from under the long boat which lies over the cook's galley amidships.

A sooty, wheezing little steamer presently takes a tow-line; the French pilot with stiff, but confident English, is at the helm; our hawser that is fast to the little tug stiffens, and we swoop away from dock and jetty; we brush a low two-master that is in our track —crash goes her boom, and our main-yard fouling in her top rigging, makes her mast bend like a withe; we upon the quarter deck shy away to avoid the falling spars; there is a creak and a slip—French oaths and English oaths mingle in the air; a broken brace spins through the whizzing blocks, until running out it falls with a splash into the water, and the little vessel is free.

I see them gathering up the fragments of their shattered boom, and catch the echo of an

angry *"Sacré!"* floating down the wind. The
jetty grows smaller; its crowds dwindle to a
black and gray patch of people, from among
whom one or two white kerchiefs are still
fluttering long and lost adieux. Presently the
mainsail is dropped; the little French pilot
screams out—"Hyst de geeb!"—the tow-rope
is slipped, and we are battling with canvas
only, for an offing, in the face of a sharp
Northwester.

My companions of the quarter-deck and
after cabin, are a young French lad who is going out to join an elder brother established in
New York—the burly captain, who makes it
a point of etiquette to appear the first day in
a new beaver which sits above his round red
face with the most awkward air in the world
—and last a Swiss lady, with three little flaxen-
haired children, who is on her way to a new
home already provided for her in the far West,
by a husband who has emigrated some previous year. It is a small company for the ample
cabin of the good ship Nimrod; but she is reputed a dull sailer; and we embark at a season
when strong westerly winds are prevailing.

The captain is a testy man, loving his power
—not so much by reason of any naturally ty-
rannic disposition, as by a long education—from

the day when he first bore the buffetings of a cabin boy,—toward the belief that authority was most respected when most despotically urged; and very much subsequent observation has confirmed me in the opinion, that many American ship-masters have brutalized all their more humane instincts, by the same harsh education of the sea.

The French lad was at that wondering, and passive age, which accepted all the accidents of his new experience of life, as normal conditions of the problem he was bound to solve; and I think that if the steward had some day killed the captain and taken command, he would have reckoned it only the ordinary procedure on American packets, and have eaten his dinner —of which he always showed high appreciation—with his usual appetite.

The Swiss lady was of a different stamp; refined and gentle to a charm; a Swiss protestant, devoted to her faith, and giving type of a class, that is I think hardly to be found out of Scotland, New England, and certain portions of Switzerland;—a class of women, with whom a sense of Christian duty—so profound as to seem almost a mental instinct—holds every action and hap in life under subordination. I paint no ascetic here, who is lashed to dogmas, and carries always a harsh Levitical judgment under lifted eyebrows; but one— slow to condemn, yearning to approve;—true as steel to one faith, but tolerant of others;— wide in sympathy, and with a charity that glows and spends, because it cannot contain itself. I wish there were more such.

The children are fairy little sprites, edu- cated, as such a mother must needs educate them—to moderate their extravagances of play, at a word, and to cherish an habitual re- spect for those older than themselves.

The first mate is a simpleton, shipped upon the last day at Havre (the old mate having slipped his birth), in whom, it is soon evi- dent, the captain has no confidence, and who becomes a mere supernumerary among the crew. The place of second mate, is filled by a sailor, who has acted as third mate; the old "second," being killed not long before by a blow from the windlass. Among the crew I note only a shy Norwegian who is carpenter, and a lithe, powerful mulatto,—with a constant protest in his look against the amalgamation of his blood,—who acts as ship's cook.

There is a tall unshaven emigrant, who brings on deck every day a sick infant wrapped in a filthy blanket, out of which the little eyes stare vividly, as if they already looked upon the scenes of another world. There is a tall singer, in a red cap—who smokes, as it seems to me, all the day long; and every pleasant evening, when the first bitter rocking of the voyage is over, he leads off a half score of voices in some German chant, which carries over the swaying water a sweet echo of the Rhineland.

There is a German girl of some eighteen summers, blue-eyed, and yellow-haired, who as she sits upon one of the water-casks, with her knitting in hand, coquettes with the tall singer; she knits—he smokes; her eyes are on her work—his eyes are upon her; she changes her needles, and looks—anywhere but at him; he fills his pipe, and looks (for that brief interval) anywhere but at her.

All these figures and faces come back to me, clear as life—as I follow the limnings of my musty note-books.

Again, on some day of storm, I see the decks drenched and empty. The main and fore top-sails are close reefed, and all others furled. The atmosphere is a wide whirl of spray, through which I see the glittering broad sides of great blue waves bearing down upon us, and buoying the flimsy ship up in mid air, as if our gaunt hulk, with all her live freight, and all her creaking timbers, were but a waif of thistle-down. Sailors in dreadnaughts grope their way here and there, clinging by the coils that hang upon the belaying pins, and "taughtening," in compliance with what seems the needless orders of the testy captain, some slackened sheet or tack. I see the deck slipping from under me as I walk, or bringing me to sudden, dreary pause, as the bow lifts to some great swell of water. And below, when I grope thither, and shut the state-room door to windward with a terrible lift, I sink back with one hand fast in the berth-curtains, and the other in the bottom of the washbowl. I reflect a moment, and try to catch the guage of the ship's movements; but while I reflect, a great plunge flings me down against the laboring door; I grasp the knob; I grasp the bed curtains which stretch conveniently toward me. The door flies open, the curtains fly back, and I am thrown headlong into my berth.

There, I can at least brace myself; now I am wedged one way; now I am wedged the other. The stifling odor of the damp clothes, the swaying curtains, the poor lamp toiling in its socket to find some level, are very wearisome and sickening. I hear noises from neighbor berths that are no way comforting; I hear feeble calls for the steward;—bah! shall I read these notes only to revive the odium of sea-sickness?

Again, I see the sun on a great reach of level water, that has only a wavy tremor in it—as peaceful as the bowing and the lifting of grain in the wind. The yellow-haired German is at her knitting; her red-capped admirer is filling his pipe. Our quarter-deck's company are all above board, and luxuriating in the charming weather—when a lank, hatless, bearded man strides with a quaint woollen bundle in his arms to the lee gangway, and "plash"—goes his burden upon the water. It is a sudden and sorry burial; for it is the dead infant, whose eyes looked beyond us, three days ago. I see the Swiss lady, with her hands met together; and her little ones, when they learn what has befallen, grow pale, and leave their play, and whisper together, and look over astern where the white bundle goes whisking under the inky blue.

Even the French lad bestirs himself into asking what it may be?

"A child—dead—that 's the body."

"*Sacr-ré!*" and he, taking his cigar from his mouth, looks after it too,—shadowy now, and fading in the depths. There are times when the weakest of us, as well as the strongest, eagerly strain our eyes and our thought toward that great mystery of Death.

It is but a shabby funeral, as I said; no prayer save the silent one of the Swiss lady. God only knows what worshipful or tender thought of the child's future, was in the mind of the emigrant father, as he tossed the little package from him into the sea. He staggered as he walked back to the hatchway, to climb below; but it may have been only from the motion of the ship.

After this—it was perhaps a matter of two days—I remember a somewhat worthier burial. It is an old man of seventy (they said) takes the plunge. He has been ailing from the day of sailing;—going with his daughter and grandchild to try the new land. She is chief-mourner. There is a plank the carpenter has brought; and he has placed one end upon the bulwarks and the other upon a cask; they lay presently a long canvas bundle upon it; the old dead man is safely sewed in, with a cannon shot at his feet. Some one among the emigrants reads a guttural prayer. The captain pops out an "Amen!" that sounds like a military command; and thereupon the carpenter, with the second-mate, tilt the plank; and away the old man slides with a sudden, heavy splash. The daughter rushes to the gangway with a scream—as if they had done him wrong, and looks yearningly after him. If she saw anything, it was only the gray sack going down—full three fathoms under, before our stern had licked the little whirlpool smooth, where he sank.

I observe after some days, that the captain is growing more crotchety and testy; it irks him to share the night watches as he does, with only the plucky little second-mate, who, though sailorly enough in his air, has I notice a very awkward handling to his sextant; but he makes up for his lack of the science of navigation with a pestilent shower of suggestions to the helmsman: "A pint nigher the wind!" "Kip her full!" "Now you 're off, you lubber!" Thus I hear him, hour after hour, as he paces off his night watches upon the deck above my head.

I look back upon a sunny noon shining down upon the vessel, and upon the little Swiss children, who have forgotten the dead baby, and are rollicking up and down the decks with glee. The mother seated by the taff-rail, with a book under her eye—is not reading, but looking over the page at that romp of her little ones—to which I have contributed my own quota, by joining in their play of "Puss in the corner."

Suddenly there is a swift, angry outcry from the waist of the ship—the sound of a quick blow—a scuffle, and loud shouts. The little children cower away like frighted deer, and the mother swoops forward, her face full of terror, to give them the protection of those outstretched arms. I step to the little bridge that reaches from the quarter deck to the long boat. There is an excited, clamorous group of sailors and of emigrants below me; in the middle of them is the captain, hatless and panting, and with his hand streaming with blood; the tall mulatto cook confronts him, his face livid with rage. I learn about the happening of it all, afterward. It seems that the captain had given an order, which the cook has chosen either to neglect, or to treat with indifference. "But by ——, sir, on my ship, sir, I'll have my orders obeyed:"—and thereupon, he has seized a billet of wood (an ugly stick, I remember,) and rushed upon the mulatto. The blow it seems only stunned the man for a moment, for he has rallied so far as to give an answering blow; and as the captain springs forward to seize him by the throat, he has caught his hand in his teeth (they are as white and sharp as a leopard's) and nearly torn away his thumb. There is a manifest show of sympathy with the mutineer, on the part of the sailors; but the instinct of obedience is strong —strong even in the culprit; for he makes no resistance now, as the carpenter and second-officer place the irons on his wrists. And presently he is safe in the meat house, under the jolly boat; at least we think so—and the captain, as well—who coolly pockets the key.

It is a sad break-in upon our quiet life of the decks; we are as yet only mid-way over the ocean, and a war is brooding on shipboard; the sailors go sulkily to their tasks; they even bandy words with the doughty second officer. Who knows what course the helmsman may give the ship to-night?

The poor Swiss lady is in an agony of apprehension, with those frighted little ones demanding explanations she cannot give. "And what if he had killed *monsieur le capitaine?— ah par exemple! Et comme il était féroce! je l'ai vu—moi.*"

I am with the watch till midnight; all is quiet; I leave the captain on deck with his arm in its sling—not the less testy, for that mangled hand of his. At four, he goes below again (so they tell me), but I am sleeping at last; yet only for a little while, and in a disturbed way.

At six, I hear a sudden rush of feet over my head, and directly after a leap down the companion way; a man bursts into the captain's room next me; I am wide awake now.

"For God's sake! quick, captain; the door is broken down, and the man's out—irons off; they say he 's armed."

I dress hurriedly; but the captain is before me, and I hear the click of his pistol-lock before he goes out.

I am all ears now for the least sound.

"There 's the scoundrel! quick!"

Whose voice is that? A tempest of oaths succeeds, and now—crack!—crack!—two pistol shots, and a heavy fall upon the deck. I rush up the companion way, and run to the quarter rail; a half-dressed swarm of emigrants are beating off the sailors, and stamp furiously upon the mulatto who is struggling, and writhing upon the deck.

The carpenter and second officer are assisting the captain to rise, and he staggers aft—not shot, but horribly bruised and scalded about the head. He has fired two shots—both, strangely enough, missed his man; and if the emigrants had not been near, the enraged cook, armed as he was with a heavy iron skillet, would have made an end of him.

The mutineer is in irons again, and is presently led aft to the taffrail, that he may have no communication with the sailors. But it is a small ship, after all, in which to pack away so resolute and determined a mutineer, against all chance of connivance. The man is suffering fearfully from that stamping of the deck;—no creature could be more inoffensive than the poor fellow now. I venture a private talk with him, and a show of some friendliness touches him to the quick.—Aye, there are those who will shiver and groan (*he* told me this) when they hear that he has worn manacles and must go to prison (he knows that); his father is alive and an honest working-man,—God help him! but his father's son never was struck a blow before. "I wish to——I 'd killed him!"

We made a common duty on the quarter-deck of dressing the captain's head, and of keeping by him during his watches. A very dreary time it was.

The carpenter reports certain oak plank, with which presently he sets to work upon a cell for the culprit, between decks, among the emigrants; and there he was lodged next day. But the sailors found their way to him, we learned; duty was more slackly performed than ever, and a thousand miles or more still between us and our Western harbor. I felt sure that if he escaped again, the prisoner would throttle the captain, as a wild beast might, and kill him out of hand. The second officer beside being a doubtful navigator, had no mettle in him to keep in awe that sullen company of sailors; I think they would have tossed him overboard; and we, of the quarter-deck, I think were not looked upon with great favor. Even the little children took on a gloomy, apprehensive air, which they may well have caught from the distraught and anxious manner of the mother.

Week follows week, and still the winds baffle us: we count thirty-five days, and six hundred miles are to be run: we listen nervously for all unusual night-sounds coming from below. The solitary pair of pistols belonging to the whole quarter-deck company are charged with four heavy slugs each. The captain meantime is threatened with erysipelas, and is compelled to keep mostly on deck; he fairly dozes upon his long watches, while the French lad or myself keep guard.

INTRODUCTION

"God send good wind!"—how we pray that prayer; but none so fervently, I am sure, as our Swiss friend, with her little jewels clustering about her.

I see the same good ship Nimrod, stanch and safe, sailing up through the Narrows, with a laughing sun playing on the shores, and three laughing and rejoicing children—looking eagerly out, at the strange sights—at the forts that flank us—at the broad bay that blazes in the front—at the islands that sleep upon its bosom—at our city spires that glitter along the horizon.

I see the manacled man brought up from below the hatches—sallow and with cavernous cheeks, and something dangerous in his eye still; he is led away between two officers to jail—to prison;—three years of it, the papers said. The French lad has eaten his last lunch, and comes upon the deck a perfect D'Orsay in his equipment. Now, he must have grown out of my knowledge; ten—twelve—fifteen years—will have given him—if dyspepsia did not make him a victim—the figure of an alderman. I trust he takes life serenely.

Is the captain among the living? Does anybody answer? And does he keep the same rotund face and form, and affect the same preposterous beaver on days of embarkation which he wore in the old times—

" as he sailed—as he sailed " ?

And the Swiss lady? She found her home —I know that—with all her flock; from her own hand, I have it:

—*"Nous y entrons avec courage et confiance, nous attentons à Celui qui a promis d'être avec nous jusqu'à la fin. Son Amour est le seul qui puisse suffire à tous nos besoins."* The same brave Christian spirit! the same hearty benevolence too:—*"Puissiez-vous, mon cher Monsieur, l'éprouver [son Amour] au plus profond de votre être afin que vous soyez heureux, selon le vœu de*

"Votre Amie."

Long years, and I heard nothing more: at length, upon a certain summer's day, I met one who knew and appreciated her sterling worth —her tender, womanly nature.

"And how is it with Madame in the new home?"

"Monsieur!——elle est au ciel!"

I believed him—with all my heart.

. . . .

INTRODUCTION

Thus far, and with a pleasant recollection of old scenes, I have but filled in the little skeleton notes that meet my eye in the musty memoranda of travel. Through all the night, I might plague my brain, and vex my heart, with this revival of scenes and characters, half forgotten, but which, when they come with that fresh and airy presence, that the small hours "ayont the twal" alone can give them, cheat me into a glow or a tenderness of feeling, of which next morning I am ashamed.

Yet why?

Our life is not all lived by day-light. It is not all summed up in what we do, or in what we shall do; what we think and what we remember, have their place in the addition. Therefore when night comes again, and when reading and severer work is done, I rather incline to build away, upon the scaffoldings which old notes and old letters may afford—story by story: and it is precisely this, which I have been doing here; until at last I have a book, Seven Stories high—to which this introduction shall serve for Basement.

FIRST STORY

WET DAY AT AN IRISH INN

FIRST STORY

On the 24th of December, 18—, I woke up at half past five in the old town of Armagh, near the north-east coast of Ireland. The day was lowery, the inn at which I was quartered, dirty and unattractive; my lonely breakfast in the coffee-room upon half-cooked chops and cold muffins—dismal in the extreme; so that I determined to brave all chances of the weather, and book myself for an outside place (all the insides being taken from Dungannon) on the coach for Drogheda. This left me, however, a spare half hour in which to ramble over the dreary old cathedral of Armagh, which my usher assured me "all the gintlemen allowed to be the oldest in the kingdom;" and another half hour, for an examination of the unfinished arches of the new cathedral, which the same veracious usher affirmed, would be "the foinest building in all Europe."

I hope it is finished before this, and that

43

under its roof, my Irish cicerone may have repented of his sins of exaggeration.

The Drogheda mail-coach in those days passed through the towns of Newry and Dundalk; and long before we had reached the first of these, which we did at about eleven of the forenoon, the cold mists had given way to a pelting rain, and I had determined to give up my fare, and risk such hospitality as an Irish inn would afford. Black's coach tavern in Newry did not promise large cheer; the front was dingy; the street narrow; the entrance hall low and begrimed with dirt and smoke. Patrick took my portmanteau to number six, and I begged for a private parlor with fire, where I might dry my wet clothes at my leisure. A gaunt woman in black, not uncommunicative, and who appeared to unite in herself the three-fold offices of landlady, maid, and waiter, showed me presently to the "Wellington" on the second floor; and Patrick was directed to kindle a fire in the rusty grate.

The apartment was not such an one as I would have chosen for a merry Christmas eve. For furniture, there was a faded and draggled carpet, a few cumbrous old chairs set off with tattered brocade, an ancient piano in the corner, a round dining table (whose damask cover showed a multitude of ink-stains,) as well as a "Dublin Mail" of the last week, and a County Gazetteer. The solitary window was hung with sombre curtains of woollen stuff, and by great good fortune looked directly upon the main street of Newry. At least, then, I might count upon the solace of studying the passers by, and possibly my opposite neighbors.

The first object, however, was to dry my wet clothes; nor was this easy; the coals were damp and did not burn freely; the chimney was foul, and there was a strong bituminous aroma presently floating through the room. But I met the situation courageously, thrust an old chair fairly between the jambs, sat myself bestride it, unfolded the yellow "Dublin Mail" over the back, and entered valorously upon a conquest of the twenty-four hours, which lay between me and the next up-coach for Drogheda. The "Dublin Mail" was dull; there was a long discussion of the Maynooth College and its regimen; but who cared for Maynooth? There was "important news from Calcutta," but I had read it in Liverpool a week before: there was a column upon American affairs, in the course of which a careful consideration of the military career of General Fillmore—this was interesting, but short. There was a murder or two mentioned in retired country districts, of landlords, or bailiffs, neither of which possessed much novelty; there was a warm editorial, ending with a resonant period about "College Green," and a little poem in a corner, written to the air of "Eirie go bragh." I laid down the "Mail" and took up the Gazetteer. I read, and felt my coat; and read again—sometimes thumbing the sweaty leaves backward, sometimes forward—in such unceasing way, however, that before my clothes were fairly dry, I could have passed an examination upon the condition and prospects of Newry, and Armagh, and Portadown.

After this recreation by the grate, I betook myself to the window. The rain was still falling in torrents. Over opposite was a watchmaker's shop, with a curiously-faced clock over the door-way, which I am sure must have hung there a score of years, and I venture to say, it is hanging there yet. Within the window of this shop, which was full of gewgaws, I caught glimpses of an old "Heriot," with a magnifier thrust into the socket of his eye, and squinting curiously over a medley of brazen cog-wheels; he looked, for all the world, as a watch-maker might do, in a country-town of New England; and I dare say, if

I had stepped over to him with my watch to mend, he would have popped it open in the same unvarying way—glanced at the trade-mark—squinted at the cogs, and thrust in some long steel feeler, and closed it with a pop, and removed his one-horned eye, and hung the watch at the end of a row of invalid watches, and promised it on Saturday, and had it ready on the Thursday following.

A little farther down the street, was the establishment of an Irish milliner; its lower windows so bedizened with bonnets and haberdashery, that I could see nothing beside—except once a pair of black eyes peeping out after a carriage that whirled by in the rain. On the other side of the goldsmith's, was the shop of a baker and pastry cook, which was decked prettily with evergreens, and within which I saw a stout woman with arms akimbo, staring out as gloomily as myself at the rain.

Over the goldsmith's shop was a window at which I saw from time to time a pair of little rosy-faced girls, who may have been seven or eight; and between them, and seemingly on most familiar terms, a tall Newfoundland dog, who appeared as much interested as themselves, in occasional, furtive glances upon the reeking street. Once or twice too, a simply dressed young woman of uncertain age, who may have been the mother of the children, showed herself at the same window.

After making these observations, and pacing up the parlor once or twice, I betook myself again to the Gazetteer. Twelve, one, two,—sounded from the clock over the mantel: two hours yet to my dinner.

Again I turned to the street for relief: a little girl, in close hood, was stepping out of the door-way beside the jeweller's shop, and, with her, the dog I had seen above stairs, with a basket in his mouth; away they went, trotting familiarly out of sight down the street; this at least was an incident for me, and I sat myself composedly down to watch for their return. The little girl's mate in the window opposite, seemed bent upon the same object. After twenty minutes perhaps, dog and child came trotting back, thoroughly drenched;— the dog still carrying the basket, now apparently weighty with some burden. And the servant happening in at the moment to look after my fire, I called her attention to the drenched couple, as they entered the door-way opposite.

"Oh, aye, surr, it 's a good baste, is that; he keeps by the poor little craythurs night and day; it 's very poor they must be, and their mither 's a lone woman; she 's been opposite a matter of three months now in a little room she 's rinted o' the gold-bater; it 's not much in the way of niddle-work she 'll be foinding; the Lord knows how the poor craythur lives."

By this time the pair had returned to their chamber, as I judged by the movements of the little girl who had been stationed at the window. Very likely she was dancing over the contents of the basket.

"Perhaps the dog has brought them their Christmas dinner," said I.

"And shure, surr, I hope he may: but it 's a sorry dinner they have most days."

A sudden thought struck me. I was out of all reach of the little Christmas charities of home; what if I were to turn a few pennies to the cheer of my little neighbors over the way? A charitable thought is best closed with at once: it is too apt to balk us, if we wait: so I pulled out a five shilling piece, and said, "My good woman, you see the cake-shop yonder?"

"And shure I do, surr."

"Would you be good enough to step over and buy a couple of little Christmas cakes, with a sprig of holly in each of them, and take them over to the two poor girls opposite, and tell them that a stranger who is rain-bound in the opposite inn, wishes them a merry Christmas for to-morrow?"

"Shure I will, surr; and the Lord bless you for 't."

There was something in the manner of the gaunt waiting woman, that forbade my doubting her: still I watched—saw her brave the rain—saw her appear with the package, saw her enter the low passage opposite, and presently the two little girls came romping to the window, and kissed their hands to me; while the mother appears for a moment with a modest bow of acknowledgment.

I think the fire burned more cheerfully after this; the room seemed to wear a new aspect; my clothes were thoroughly dry; my appetite was ripening for dinner; and I read the little poem in the corner of the "Dublin Mail" to the air of "Eirie go bragh" with a good deal of kindliness.

The waiting woman, with grateful messages, had come and gone, and I was deep in Maynooth again, when my attention was called by the rattle of a carriage in the street. It had apparently come to a stop near by. I strolled to the window to see how it might be. Sure enough, over opposite was an Irish jaunting car all mud-bespattered, two portmanteaus upon it, and a stout, ruddy-faced man in mackintosh, and in close-fitting skull cap, just alighting. He stepped into the goldsmith's shop, apparently to make some inquiries—seemed satisfied on the instant— returned to the car, ordered off the portmanteaus, and pulled out his purse—a well-filled one I judged—to pay the driver. The little girls I noticed were pressing their faces against the glass and gazing down—once or twice looking back as if to summon their mother to the scene. She also appeared presently (it was just as the drenched traveller had paid his fare, and had raised his face), and looking earnestly for a moment—drooped away, and fell, beside the window. There could be no doubt that the woman had fainted; there was terror in the faces of the children.

I rang the bell hastily, and stepping to the door as the waitress came, I said, "My good woman, there 's trouble over the way; the mother of those children has just swooned by the window, and there 's no one to care for her."

She came forward to look out, with true womanly curiosity, though there was no hope of seeing what the actual trouble might be.

There was a vain glance at the opposite chamber, then her eye fastened on the newly-arrived traveller, who was busy yet with his portmanteaus.

"Good God," said she, in consternation, "it 's Moike Carlingford! Yes, by the powers, it 's Moike," and she clasped her hands together, in what I thought a most melodramatic way for a woman of her age, and presence.

"It 's naught but Moike," said she again, as if appealing to me. "He was niver a bit lost then, and it 's he, as shure as iver I live."

"And pray who may Mike Carlingford be?" said I, thinking the matter was getting a touch of humor; but her answer brought me to a dead pause.

"Moike? why Moike is a murderer! It 's not for me to say it, but it 's the law; and I knew him as well as iver I knew my brither before he wint away, and fell to bad ways; and he wint down by Belfast, and there was an old gintleman that lived there—it 's near eight years agone—and Moike would marry his daughter or his niece, and the gintleman would n't hearken, and Moike bate the old gintleman a bit roughly, and Moike dropped his badge in the bush, where they found the old gint's body, and he got away, and they followed him to Cork, and he took ship, and the ship was lost and all aboard, and by my sowl it 's Moike again yonder, and he 'll be caught, and be hung; and I 'm sorry for Moike!"

There was a good swift Irish current in her story, and at the end of it, she rushed away to spread the news below stairs. Meantime the newly-arrived personage opposite had passed in with his luggage: there was nothing more to be observed at the window over the goldsmith's shop: children, dog, and mother had alike disappeared. I fancied I heard from time to time, an exciting discussion going on below stairs in the inn; but who were the parties to it, or what was the burden, I could not determine.

The "Dublin Mail" and the Gazetteer had now lost their interest: Mike the murderer had even driven the fainting woman opposite, wholly out of my mind. I could not for a moment doubt that there was some connection between the two parties of which the talkative landlady was ignorant. But was the mother's emotion the result of fear? Had this stout Mike reappeared to commit new crimes? I cannot say that I had the least apprehension:

the jolly face of the new-comer, with the iron-gray whiskers, and the sun-burnt cheeks, could no more be associated with the idea of murder, than the Christmas season. The good woman of the inn must be laboring under some strange mistake. Yet what right after all, had I—a passing traveller—to doubt her earnest assertion?

My wet day at the Irish inn was gaining an interest that I could not have believed possible. Time and again I looked over the way, but no living creature appeared at the window. Presently I observed the stumpy figure of my landlord moving across the street, where he entered the shop of the watch-maker, and opened an earnest conference; at least I judged as much by his extraordinary gesticulations, and by the nervous rapidity with which the old Heriot pushed aside his cog-wheels, and came fairly around his little counter to talk more freely with the visitor. I inferred from what I had seen thus far, that Mike Carlingford was a character at one time well known hereabout, that an evident mystery of some kind attached to his history, and that the host had taken over the suspicions of the mistress to compare with the observations of the old shop-keeper; I inferred farther from the resolute shakings of the head of this latter (which I plainly saw through his glass door) that the watch-mender had either not observed closely the features of the new-comer (a thing scarcely possible), or that he doubted wholly the suspicions of the acting landlady.

My host came back in an apparently disturbed and thoughtful mood. It still lacked an hour to my dinner, and the rain was unabated; a walk about the old town, which I should have been charmed to take, was not to be thought of. What if I were to make some excuse to step below to the tap-room and engage the host himself in a little talk, that might throw some light on my opposite neighbors? No sooner thought, than done. The stumpy little man was abundantly communicative. He had been engaged in the tap, and had not seen the "car" drive up. "Meesus Flaherty, she that okerpies persition as landleddy since that Mistress O'Donohue—that 's me wife, Surr, that was—is dade, has a good mimory, and thinks that it 's Moike that has come back to life. Loike enuff; if it 's indade Moike, he 'll be hung. Maybe it 's Moike, and again maybe it 's not Moike; it 's not for the like o' me to jist say. Mister Rafferty, it 's he that minnds the watches in a very pertikeler manner, and has been my neighbor for a score o' years, says, by all the powers, that it 's not Moike Carlingford at all, and he 's not for disturbin' the darlints above stairs, if so be they 're to have a merry Christmas among 'em."

I venture to ask after the murder, with which Carlingford's name had been associated.

"It 's seven or eight years gone now," said the host—"indade it 's a good bit better than that, it must be ten or twelve since Moike that lived hereabouts goes down nigh to Belfast, and they say fell into bad company there; and he was one of the younkers that took to wearin' o' badges, and the elictions were coming off, and plenty o' shindies they had. And an old gintleman—Dormont was his name—who lived jist out o' Belfast, was a tirrible politician, and was a magistrate too; it 's he was murdered. He had clapped some of the badge-boys into prison, and they threatened him; and sure enough by and by they found the poor gintleman with his skull cracked, lying in a bit of brush, at his gate. They found him in the morning, with a young pup, that he had, nosing about him, and playing with a bit o' ribbon, which, when they came to examine, was Moike Carlingford's badge, with his name in full to 't.' "

"And was this all the evidence?" I asked.

"This started the scent, as it were: but it came out at the inquest that Moike had been seen hanging about the place night after night, and what 's more he was in love with the gintleman's daughter or niece, and Dormont had forbid him the house, and threatened Moike; which Moike was n't the man to bear, without his speech back; and there were them that heard it. But what was worst of all, he was n't to be found for the trile: they traced him to Cork, where he went aboard the Londonderry that sailed for a place in Rushy, which was lost at sea and niver a man found; which, if ye plase, looks a good deal as if it 's niver Moike; though to be shure, the Flaherty has an iligant mimory."

"And what became of the poor girl?" said I.

"And shure, that 's the worst of it: she wint from thereabouts, and they say (dropping his voice) there was a little baby one day, which she said that she was married, but would niver tell who was her husband, which looked uncommon suspicious; and her father would n't take her in, and there was a story

I heard from a North of England man, where her father lived, that she went to the workus and died there."

This finished the report of the landlord, and I sauntered up again to the Wellington parlor, where the Flaherty, in a clean cap and ribbons, was just then laying the cloth.

The bustle of some new arrival called her away for a few moments; she re-appeared, however, shortly after—begging my "pardin —but there 's an Inglish gintleman just come in, and the coffee-room is not over tidy for visitors, tho' she had spoken to Mister O'Donohue times enough—and would I be so good as to allow the Inglish gintleman to share the Wellington parlor with me?"

"Of course," I said, "I shall be delighted; and if the gentleman don't think the hour too early, perhaps we can take a cut off the same joint."

The Flaherty was most gracious in her thanks. Presently the new visitor came up the stairs, attended by the landlord.

"It 's near to Armagh, you tell me?" I overheard him say.

"A matter of three miles the hither side," returned the landlord.

"You 're sure of the name,—Bonneford?"

"As shure as I am of me own."

"Very good," returned the Englishman, "have me a 'fly' at the door at seven; we 'll put two horses to the road; two hours there and two back: will you have a bed for me at midnight if I come?"

"Wheniver you loike," said the host; and the Englishman came bustling in—a tall sandy-haired man of sixty perhaps, full of restiveness, and of the condition, I should judge, of a moderately well-to-do English farmer. He wore a snuff colored coat, and over it a mackintosh,—yellow leathern gaiters, splashed with mud, and a broad-brimmed drab hat.

He thanked me for my civility in a short, sharp way, and after a very brief toilet, disposed himself for the dinner which was now smoking on the table.

"And Mary," said he turning to the gaunt landlady, "please bring me a pint o' sherry, and let Boots clean up my galoshes, and let him have the 'fly' at the door at seven to a minute; and Mary—"

"Mistress Flaherty, surr!"—with a curtsy, said the woman.

"Oh, eh, I beg pardon Mistress Flaherty; and will Mistress Flaherty see that the sheets have a good airing for me, against midnight or thereabouts,—there 's a good woman?"

"The house niver gives damp sheets, surr."

"It 's a 'igh feather these Irish maids wear in their caps," said he as the landlady disappeared.

We fell presently to discussion of the mutton, and to the relative merits of the Southdowns and of the little moor-fed sheep one meets with in Ireland, in which I found he was as thoroughly English in his tastes, as in his appearance. We talked of the bog, of the potato disease, of the poor-rates; an hour passed thus, and finally we came back to the weather and the Christmas season;—"not just the season," I observed, "that an Englishman usually chooses to while away in a damp inn."

"Quite right," said he, as he went on compounding a punch from a few fragrant materials brought up from the tap; "quite right as you say, and a damp ride on such a night as this, is worse than the inn and the punch."

This latter cheered him, and invited a more personal chat than he had yet indulged in.

"It is to Armagh you are going to-night?" said I.

"Thereabouts," said he, "and I may tell you, now that we 've tasted the punch to-

gether—your good 'elth, sir—that if I find
the man I 'm in search of, and if he 's the man
I take him for, this will be the merriest Christmas eve I 've passed in twenty years' time.''

"Indeed," said I, rather startled by a certain
pathos in his tone which I had not before recognized; "some old friend, perhaps?"

"Not a bit of it—not one bit; never saw
him in my life. The oddest thing in the
world."

This was said rather to himself than to me,
and he relapsed into a musing mood, which I
did not feel at liberty for a time to interrupt.

"It 's not the first mystery that 's perplexed
me to-day," said I, half laughingly, as the
stranger lifted his head again.

"Ah, indeed—and pray, if I may be so bold,
what 's the other?"

"Come to the window and perhaps I can
show you," said I. The December evenings
in the North of Ireland are terribly long. Our
own candles had been lighted since three of
the afternoon; and as I pulled aside the curtain, the street lamps and shop fronts were
all cheerfully ablaze. Over the watch-maker's
in the window where my chief observation
of the morning had centred there was no lamp
burning, but there was a ruddy glow in the

room, such as a well lighted grate-full of coals might throw out.

"Do you see?" said I, "over the way? There's a dog lying before the fire."

"Aye, aye,—I see."

"And there's a woman in the shadow by the hearth."

"Quite right, I can make out her figure."

"And there's a pair of children; you see how the fire-light reddens up their faces?"

"Aye, aye, chubby rogues—God bless me, I had such once. And that's the father I suppose, from the way they lean upon him and tug at his waistcoat?"

"There's the mystery," says I.

"Oho!"

"Does he look like a murderer?" said I.

"Bless my soul! murderer! What do you mean?"

I dropped the curtains, and when we had taken our places again before the fire, I detailed to him the incidents of the morning. He seemed to enjoy immensely the oddity of the whole thing, and chiefly the assurance of the gaunt old Flaherty, who brought up a murderer from the bottom of the North Sea to drive straight into town on such a dreary December day.

"But whose was this murder?" says my companion, with a sudden, thoughtful check to his hilarity.

"Dormont, was the name I think."

The man gave a sudden start. "Bless me! Ben Dormont! I began to suspect as much. Why do you know I knew him like a brother; in fact he *was* my wife's brother; and lived away here in the North of Ireland; aye, Ben Dormont; he was murdered true enough; but it's not our friend over yonder that did it. There was a story I know that some young Belfast-man killed him, and they tracked him to Cork; but he, poor fellow, went down in —the Londonderry—sure enough—the very ship; they're right there. But the man who killed Dormont was Pat Eagan, who died in Ingy three years gone. My son, you must know, is sergeant in Her Majesty's forty-third, and Pat was one of his men—enlisted in Ingy. He fell sick of the fever there, and at the last wanted a priest, and a magistrate, and made a clean breast of it. My boy sent home copies of all the papers; if the Flaherty wants them to clear up the name of her drowned friend, she shall have them."

I must confess to a strong feeling of relief at this revelation; for in spite of myself I was beginning to feel a warm interest in the people over the way, and had been oppressed with an uncomfortable sense of the Flaherty's earnestness, and of her "iligant mimory."

But there was another little episode connected with the story of the murder, as the landlord had detailed it, which perhaps my English companion might throw light upon; indeed, I had my suspicions, that he had purposely waived all allusion to it. But my curiosity overbore, for the time, all sense of delicacy.

"If I remember rightly," said I, carelessly, "there was a young woman associated in some way with the story of this Dormont murder?"

The old gentleman's face quivered; for a moment he seemed to hesitate how he should meet the question; then he broke out in a tone of passionate bitterness:

"Aye sir, you 've heard it; you 've heard she was a wanton, and I fear it was God's truth; you 've heard her father shut his door upon her, and I wish my hand had withered before I did it. You 've heard she died in the workus—God forgive me;—my daughter, sir; my poor, wretched Jane!"

Patrick tapped at the door and said the "fly" was ready.

The old gentleman sat by the fire leaning forward, and with his face buried in his hands. Presently he rose, with his composure partly restored again. "You know now," said he, approaching me, "why I 've had many a weary Christmas; but I 've a faint hope left; and I 'm in chase of it to-night. I told you my boy heard of the confession of Pat Eagan, and went to see him before he died. He told him who he was, and asked if he could tell the truth about Jane. 'Is she alive or dead?' said Pat. 'Dead,' said my boy. 'I don't know all the truth,' said Pat, 'but there 's a man in Ingy can right her name if he will; and his name is James Bonneford.' And my boy wrote me that he hunted that man through the country, as he would have hunted a deer: now he heard of him, now he did n't hear of him. There were two years or more of this, when he wrote me (and the letter only came a week ago) that the man had gone to Ireland, on his way to Ameriky; and that he might be heard of about Armagh. That 's my errand to-night."

"God help you," said I.

And he drew on his galoshes, buttoned up his mackintosh, bade me good evening, and presently I heard the fly rattling away up the street.

I stirred the fire, drew my chair before it, and was meditating another attack upon the county Gazetteer, when Patrick appeared with a slip of paper which he handed me, and says —"It 's a man below steers, as would loike a worrd with the gintleman in the Wellington parlor."

I turned the paper to the light—"James Bonneford," in a full, bold hand was written on it. It was my English companion of the dinner, doubtless, the man was in search of; but how on earth could he have got wind of his arrival? The mysteries of the day were thickening on me.

As I walked leisurely down the stairs, I overheard violent and excited talk from the tap-room; and from the chance words that caught my ear, I saw that Mistress Flaherty's suspicions of the morning were meeting active discussion. Mr. Bonneford could wait surely, until I learned what course the altercation was taking. A half dozen of the neighbors had strolled in, and among them, with a terribly excited face, I saw the object of suspicion himself.

"And who is it says Mike Carlingford's come home?" says he, challenging the company with a defiant air.

"It 's Meestress Flaherty," says one.

"Flaherty be d— !" said the man. "Did n't Mike Carlingford go down with the Londonderry, eight years ago?"

"Moike, Moike," said the Flaherty pressing forward, "don't forswear yourself, if ye did rap the old man on the head. It 's Moike ye are; and if I was hanged for it, I 'd say it, and may the Lord have mercy on ye!"

There was an earnestness and directness in the old woman's tones that carried conviction to the neighbors.

The man saw it only too clearly, and his jaw dropped; the color left his face; I thought he would have fallen; but he rallied, and said in a subdued tone—all his defiance gone—"It 's not *you* 'll be hanged, Mistress Flaherty: it 's me they 'd be afther hanging. They chased me out of Ireland, and only the Lord saved me when the Londonderry went down, and I thought shure He would have made it right before long; but He has n't. For I 'm as innocent of that murder as the babe that 's unborn."

"I belave ye, Moike," said the Flaherty; "now I look at yer and hear ye say it—by my sowl and I belave ye, Moike."

"You are quite right, I think, my good

woman," said I. And thereupon I detailed to them the particulars which I had learned from the Englishman above stairs; and I think I never made a little speech which was more approved.

"Thank God—thank God!" said Mike, while a half dozen, and the Flaherty foremost, crowded about him to give his hand a shake.

"Now, for the little woman!" said Mike, springing away.

"He was married then," said a voice.

"Aye," said Mike starting back, "who dares to say she was n't? Married a fortnight before the cursed murder; 't was that took me so often to the house; and the very night, Janey pulls away my badge, and says Mike don't be after wearing these ribbons—they 'll get you in trouble; and she threw it to Touser that was lying under the table, and the dog followed me out that night, and there, near to the gate, he found the old man, and hung by him. But Touser has made the bad job good to me; there 's niver a man or woman in Ireland or England, not excepting her own father, that 's been so kind to the children, ever since they were born, as that dog."

"Children!" says Flaherty, "and by my

sowl, I consated it long ago;—them **girrls** is twins!"

"A brace of them," said Mike, "and I never saw their blessed faces till this day noon; and now they 'll have an honest name to carry: it 's this that 's borne so hard upon the little woman: for at the very last I said to her,— "Janey, whatever befalls, mind ye wait till God clears it up, before you do the naming: it 's better a child should have none, than a murderer's." And with that, and shouting merry Christmas at all of them, Mike dashed out, and across the street again.

Of course I had forgotten all about Mr. Bonneford; I suspected who he must be; Patrick made the matter clear—"And shure it 's Moike, hisself; is n't it written—Moike?" (looking at the slip of paper in my hand). "He said he 'd be jist afther thanking the gintleman that sent over the cakes the mornin'."

"All right, Patrick; and now Patrick put some fresh coals on the fire in the 'Wellington,' and ask the Flaherty to bring me two or three sheets of paper, ink-stand and pens."

I had been writing an hour or two perhaps, when I heard the rattle of a fly below, and remembered that my dinner friend must be nearly due, on his return. In he came presently, thoroughly fagged, heart-sick, and moody.

"I am afraid you 've been unsuccessful," I said.

"My boy has been deceived," he said. "The only Bonnefords about Armagh, are a quiet family, that I went blundering upon with a story about Ingy, and James Bonneford, till I believe they thought me a mad-man; I 'm not far from it, God knows!"

"Cheer up, my good friend," said I, "a visitor has been in since you left, about whom you 'll be glad to hear;" and I tossed the strip of paper toward him. The old gentleman took out his spectacles, and spelled it letter by letter,—"*James Bonneford!*—what does all this mean?" says he in a maze.

"It means this," said I, "that James Bonneford is only the name that Mike Carlingford wore in India to escape suspicion and pursuit; and this Mike Carlingford is the legal husband of your daughter Jane (the old man's face lighted here with the gladdest smile I ever saw) and they are both now over the way, with their children (here the old man's face grew fairly radiant) and I daresay, if they knew you were here, they would invite **you** to pass Christmas eve with them."

There was dead silence for a moment.

—"No they would n't—no they would n't," fairly blubbered the old man; then turning upon me, with something of his former manner, "You 're not playing me unfair? It 's all true you are telling me?"

"As true as that you are sitting before me."

The old gentleman leaped from his chair, and made a dash into the hall—turned again, came back with his broad-brim drawn far over his brow—his lips twitching nervously, and muttering "I 've treated her like a brute—like a brute—indeed I have."

"I know you have, my good friend," said I, "and it 's quite time you began to treat her like a woman and a daughter."

"That 's what I will," said he, taking courage and moving away.

"One moment."

I wrote upon a slip of paper;—CHRISTMAS EVE IS A GOOD TIME TO FORGIVE INJURIES.— I folded it and begged him to take it across the street, with the compliments of the season from the Wellington parlor: "There was a little gift for the girls in the morning," said I, "and this is for the Papa."

I hope it may have had its effect: it is quite certain that something did; for I saw no more of my dinner companion that night; and when I looked out of my chamber window at eight o'clock next morning, who should I see upon the sunny side of the street (it had cleared over-night), but the same old gentleman, beaming with smiles, leading a little grand-child by each hand, and the dog "Touser" following after, with a very mystified air.

. And when I took the coach for Drogheda, as I did at nine, a rosy cheeked little girl came running over with a merry Christmas for me (which I met with a kiss), and a sprig of Holly tied with white ribbon, which I placed in my button hole and kept there through all that lonely ride.   At night, I transferred it to my note-book, and it is .from its crumbling leaves, lying there still, that I have fanned this little story of an Irish Christmas into shape.

SECOND STORY

ACCOUNT OF A CONSULATE

SECOND STORY

ACCOUNT OF A CONSULATE

JULIUS CÆSAR was a Consul, and the first Bonaparte; and so was I.

I do not think that I am possessed of any very extraordinary ambition. I like comfort, I like mushrooms; (truffles I do not like). I think Lafitte is a good wine, and wholesome. Gin is not to my taste, and I never attended caucuses. Therefore, I had never entertained great expectations of political preferment, and lived for a considerable period of years without any hopes in that way, and with a very honest indifference.

And yet, when my name actually appeared in the newspapers, as named by appointment of the President, Consul to —— Blank, I felt, I will confess (if I may use such an expression), an unusual expansion. I felt confident that I had become on a sudden the subject of a good deal of not unnatural envy. I excused people for it, and never thought of blaming or of resenting it. My companions in the every-day walks of life, I treated, I am satisfied, with the same consideration as before.

In short, I concealed my elation as much as possible, and only indulged the playful elasticity of my spirits in a frequent private perusal of that column of the *New York Times* which made the announcement of my appointment, and where my name appeared in print, associated with those of the distinguished Mr. Soulé, Mr. Greaves (I believe), Mr. Daniels, Mr. Brown, Mr. McCrea, and a great many others.

I cannot accurately describe my feelings when the postmaster of our town (a smart gentleman of great tact, but now turned out), handed me a huge packet from the Department of State, franked by Mr. Marcy (evidently his own hand had traced the lines), sealed with the large seal of the Department, and addressed to me, Mr. Blank, Consul of the United States for —— Blank. I took the postmaster by the hand and endeavored to appear cool. I think I made some casual remark about the weather. Good heavens, what a hypocrite!

I broke open the packet with emotion. It contained a notice (I think it was in the Secretary's hand) of my appointment to ——

Blank. It contained a printed list of foreign ministers and consuls, in which my name was entered in writing. In the next issue, I was sure it would appear in print. It contained a published pamphlet (quite thin) of instructions. It contained a circular, on paper of a blue tinge, recommending modest dress. I liked the friendly way in which the recommendation was conveyed; not absolutely compelling, but advising—a black coat, and black pantaloons. In the warmth of my grateful feelings at that time, I think I should have vowed compliance if the Secretary had advised saffron shorts, and a sky-blue tail-coat.

There was, beside, in the packet a blank of a bond, to be filled up in the sum of two thousand dollars, as a kind of guarantee for the safe return of such consular property as I might find at —— Blank. I was gratified at being able to render such a substantial evidence of my willingness to incur risks for the sake of my country, and of the Administration. It was necessary, however, that two good bondsmen should sign the instrument with me. I knew I should have no difficulty in finding them. I asked two of my friends to come forward in the matter. They came forward promptly; and without an *arrière-*

pensée (to make use of an apt foreign expression) they put their names to the bond. I should be tempted to give their names here, did I not know their modesty would be offended by public notice.

I sent the instrument to Washington in a large envelope, with a mention in one corner, in my own hand-writing,—"*Official Business.*" I did not drop it into the outside box of the offiee, but presented it with my own hands through the trap to the clerk. The clerk read the address, and turned toward me with a look of consideration that I never saw upon his face before. And yet (so deceitful is human pride), I blew my nose as if nothing of importance had happened! I knew that the clerk would mention the circumstance of the "Official" letter to the second clerk, and that both would look at me with wonder when they next met me in the street, or gazed on me in my pew at the church. In short, I cannot describe my feelings.

A few days after, I received one or two letters in handwriting unknown to me; they proved to be applications for clerkships in my consular bureau. I replied to them in a civil, but perhaps rather stately manner, informing the parties that I was not yet aware of the actual income of the office, but if appearances were favorable, I promised to communicate further.

A friend suggested to me that perhaps, before assuming so important a trust, it would be well to make a short trip to the seat of government, and confer personally with the members of the Cabinet. The suggestion seemed to me judicious. I should in this way be put in possession of the special views of the Administration, and be better able to conduct the business of my office, in agreement with the Government views of international policy, and the interests of the world generally. It is true, the cost of the journey would be something, but it was not a matter to be thought of in an affair of so grave importance. I therefore went to Washington.

In a city where so many consuls are (I might say) annually appointed, it was not to be expected that my arrival would create any unusual stir. Indeed it did not. If I might be allowed the expression of opinion on such a point, I think that the inn-keeper gave me a room very near the roof—for a consul. I called almost immediately on my arrival at the office of the Secretary of State. I was told that the Secretary of State was engaged, but was recommended by his door-keeper to enter my name at the bottom of a long list in his possession, in order that I might secure my turn for admittance. I represented my official character to the door-keeper. I could not discover that his countenance altered in the least; he, however, kindly offered to present me at the door of the consular bureau.

The gentlemen of that department received me graciously, and congratulated me, I thought, in a somewhat gleeful manner, considering their responsible positions, upon my appointment. At my request they showed me some communications which were on file from the consular office I was destined to fill. There were a few letters on foolscap, and a few on note paper. They did not seem to me to come up altogether to the "Instructions." I made a remark to that effect, which appeared to be unobserved.

Among other papers was a list of the effects belonging to the consular office at —— Blank. It read, if I remember rightly:

"One Small Flag.

"One Brass Stamp.

"One Pewter do.

"Two Books of Record.

"Nine Blank Passports.

"One broken-legged Table.

"Two Office Stools (old).

"One 'Arms' (good condition)."

I must say I was surprised at this list. It seemed to me there was some discrepancy between the two thousand dollar bond I had signed, and the value of the effects of which I was to come into possession. It seemed to me, however, that furniture and things of that sort might be dear in so distant a country. I had no doubt they were. I hinted as much to the clerk in attendance.

He said he thought they might be.

"*Nous verrons*," said I, at which he smiled and said, "Oh, you know the language, then?"

I said I should know it; only the place was Italian, and the remark I had just made was in the French language.

"Oh dear, well," said he, "I don't think it makes any difference."

I told him "I hoped it would n't."

"It 's rare they know the language," said he, picking a bit of lint off from his coat-sleeve.

I felt encouraged at this.

"Only take a small dictionary along," continued he.

I asked if there was one belonging to the offiee?

He thought not.

I asked him, then, how much he thought the place was worth?

At this he politely showed me an old account of "returns." It seemed to be a half-yearly account, though some of the half-years were skipped apparently, and the others, I really thought, might as well have been skipped. Indeed I was not a little taken aback at the smallness of the sums indicated. I daresay I showed as much in my face, for the clerk told me, in a confidential way, that he doubted if the returns were full. He thought they might be safely doubled. I thought, for my own part, that there would not be much safety in doubling them even.

The clerk further hinted, that within a short time such positions would be of more value; there was to be a revisal of the consular system.

I told him I had heard so; as, indeed, I had, any time and many times within the last ten or fifteen years. Beside which—there was my country!

" Breathes there a man with soul so dead"

(to quote a popular piece of poetry), who would not serve his country, even if the fees are small?

And again, the returns were doubtless misrepresented: indeed, I had heard of a private boast from a late incumbent of the post, to the effect that "he had lived in clover." I had no doubt, in my own mind, that the Government had, in some way, paid for the clover.

I was disappointed, finally, in respect to an interview with the Secretary of State. I had the honor, however, while at Washington, of a presentation to the Under-Secretary. I do not think that he was aware of my appointment, or, indeed, that he had ever heard of me before; though he made a kind effort to recall me to remembrance; and, in any event was pleased (he said) to make my acquaintance. He expressed himself to the effect that men of character were needed for Government offices.

I told him I thought they were.

The instructions ordered that I should give information to the Department of the time of my sailing for my foreign destination, with the name of the port at which I was to embark, and of the ship. This I did—as the instructions enjoined—upon foolscap. I must not omit to mention, that I was provided with a special passport—not, indeed, bearing the usual insignia of the eagle and darts, but an

autograph passport, designating in good English my rank and destination, and inviting
foreign Governments generally to show me
the attention due to my official capacity.

I put this in my portmanteau, together with
a pocket edition of VATTEL *On the Law of
Nations*, for private reference, and also a
small dictionary. With these, I bade my
friends adieu, shaking them cheerfully by the
hand, and from the poop of the ship waved
a farewell to my country. The professed
travel-writers—such as Bayard Taylor—describe these things a great deal better. I can
only say that, with a very bitter feeling in my
chest, I went below, where I remained the
most of the time until we reached the other
side.

When I arrived in France—where I was
not personally known—I trusted very much
to the extraordinary passport which I carried,
and which I had no doubt would make considerable impression upon the officials. Indeed, a timid man who had made the voyage
with me, and who was in some way made
aware of my consular capacity (though I
never hinted it myself,) ventured to hope that
I would give him my assistance in case his
papers were not all right. I promised I would

do so. I may say that I felt proud of the application.

I walked with great confidence into the little receiving-room of the police, guided by two soldiers who wore caps very much like a reversed tin-kettle, and presented my special passport. The chief of the office looked at it in a very hard manner, and then passed it to his neighbor. I was certainly prepared for a look of consideration on their part. On the contrary, I thought they examined me with a good deal of impertinent scrutiny.

At length one of them said, with an air of confidence, *"Vous êtes Anglais?"*—You are English?

I could not help saying—using the French form of expression—*"Mon Dieu!*—no!"

And I proceeded to tell him what I really was, and that the passport was an American passport, and of an official character. The officers looked at it again, and seemed to consult for a while together; at length one said, *"C'est égal*—it 's all the same"—asked me my name, and, with some hesitation, placed his seal upon the instrument. In this way I was let into France. The timid man who had voyaged with me, had, meantime, sidled away. I suspect he must have gone up to Paris by an early train, for I did not meet with him again. I hope he had no trouble.

There was not very much made of my dignity in any part of France; but not being accredited to that country, I felt no resentment, and enjoyed Paris perhaps as much as any merely private citizen could do. To prevent, however, any mistake in future about my passport, I printed in large characters and in the French language, upon the envelope, "Passport of Blank, Consul of the United States of America, for —— Blank."

This was a good hit, and was, I found, readily understood. The landlord, with whom I staid while in Paris (an obliging man) made up his bill against the title in full. It was pleasant to have recognition.

I continued my journey in excellent spirits. I think it was on the road through Switzerland that I fell in with a chatty personage in the *coupé* of the diligence; and having at one time to hand my passport to a soldier at a frontier station, the paper came under the eye of my companion of the *coupé*. He was charmed to have the honor of my acquaintance. He expressed an excessive admiration for my country and my fellow-members of the Government.

I asked him if he had ever been in the United States? He said he had not; but he had a friend, he told me, who once touched at Guadaloupe, and found the climate delightful.

I told him, in all kindness, that the United States did not reach as far as that.

"*Comment?*" said he.

I repeated, that at the time I left, the West Indies were not included in the United States.

"*Oh, çà arrivera!*" said he; and he made a progressive gesture with his two hands, as if he would embrace the flank of the diligence horses.

He asked me if the country was generally flat?

I told him it was a good deal so.

"But, *mon Dieu!*" said he, "what fevers and steamboats you have—*vous avez là bas!*"

In short, he proved a very entertaining companion; and upon our arrival at the station of the Customs, he presented me, with a good deal of ceremony, to the presiding officer as the Consul of the United States. It was the first time (indeed, one of the few times) upon which I had received official recognition. The Customsman bowed twice, and I bowed twice in return. The presentation proved very serviceable to me, as it was the means of relieving me from a very serious difficulty shortly after.

My passport, as I have already remarked, was wholly in manuscript; and the only characters at all conspicuous in it were those which made up the name of "WM. L. MARCY." I do not mean to attribute to that gentleman the vanity of wishing to appear more important than the Consul, even in the instrument with which I was fortified. But the truth was, that the Secretary of State's signature, being in his stout autograph, was quite noticeable in contrast with the light, clerkly flourishes by which it was surrounded.

In short, it was presumed at the guardhouse that my papers gave protection—if they gave protection to anybody (which seems to have been doubted)—to Mr. Wm. L. Marcy. I was entered, therefore, upon the police record under that name. But on discovery of the fact that my luggage bore a different address, it was further presumed that Mr. Marcy had purloined the effects of another party; and under this apprehension, I came very near being placed in confinement.

I explained the matter eagerly, but had considerable difficulty in making the officials understand that I was really not Mr. Marcy;

and not being Mr. Marcy, could not be accused of any misdeeds attributable to that gentleman. I furthermore explained, as well as I was able, that Mr. Marcy was a *grand homme* (and here the French came gracefully to my aid)—that he was, in short, a man of great distinction—highly esteemed in the country from which I came, and absolutely retained there by his official duties, making it utterly impossible for him to be travelling just now upon the Continent of Europe, even with his own luggage—setting aside the calumny of his having taken possession of another man's.

I fear, however, that all would have been of no avail, if the Customsman had not been sent for, and had not come gallantly to my relief. I was indebted to him—under Providence—for my escape.

Upon arrival at my port of destination, I was evidently regarded with considerable suspicion. In common with some fifty others, I was packed in a small barrack-room until decision should be had upon our papers of admission. After very much earnest study of my passport, both within and without, the chief of the examining department (who was a scholarly man deputed for that employment) seemed to understand that I had come in the professed quality of Consul.

He asked me, in a solemn tone, if the fact was as he had surmised?

I told him, eagerly, that he was quite correct.

Upon this he gave me a ticket of admission, authorizing me to enter the town, and advising me to apply in two days' time at the bureau of police for my passport or a permit of residence.

I took lodgings at a respectable hotel, and was presently found out by a shrewd fellow (a Swiss, I think), who executed the languages for the house. He wished to know if I would like to engage him for "the sights."

I replied in a playful way—disguising as much as possible my dignity—that I was to stop some time; that I was, in short, Consul for the United States, and should probably have many leisure opportunities.

He felt sure I would. He took off his hat, and showed tokens of respect for the office which I never met with before—nor since.

I beg to recommend him to any party travelling in that direction; his name is, I think, Giacomo Guarini; aged forty-five, and broad in the shoulders, with a slight lisp in his English.

By his advice I called at the bureau of the police, where I made known my quality of Consul. They were sorry, the officials said, that they had no information of that kind. I expressed some surprise, and stated that I had the honor to bring the information myself— alluding to the passport.

They observed that, though this information was very good for me, as coming from *my* Government, it was hardly so good for them, who awaited all such information from *their* Government. Not having yet consulted Vattel very thoroughly, I did not deem it prudent to reply hastily to this first diplomatic proposition. If, indeed, there had been an eagle on the passport——!

The officials informed me that, if I wished to stay in the town, I could do so by paying ten *Zwanzigers* (about a dollar and a half our money) for a permit.

I asked how it would be if I purchased no such permit?

In that case I must leave (though it was very kindly expressed).

I reflected that, all things considered, it would be better to stay. My experience with my passport, thus far, had not been such as to warrant any great reliance on that instrument.   Indeed, I think I should advise a friend anticipating travel (for pleasure), to provide himself with a private passport.

This point being settled, I looked over my official papers and found a letter addressed by the Secretary of State to the "Present Incumbent" of the office, requesting him to deliver into my keeping the seals, flags, stools, and arms of the office.

I made inquiries regarding him.   Nobody about the hotel seemed to know him, or, indeed, ever to have heard of him.   I had fortunately a private letter to a banker of the town (exceedingly useful to me afterward).   I called upon him, and renewed my inquiries. He regretted, he said, to inform me that Mr. ——, the late acting Consul, had only the last week committed suicide by jumping out of his office-window into the dock.

I must confess that I was shocked by this announcement.   I hoped it was not owing to any embarrassments arising out of his official position.   The banker, who was a polite man, regretted that he could not inform me.

I must not omit to mention that the letter of the Secretary of State, requesting the supposed incumbent to deliver up the papers, the seals, the stools, etc., contained (through some error of the clerk) the name of some other person than myself as the proper recipient; so that I had, from the time of my landing in Europe, entertained considerable doubt about the success of my application. It was then with a feeling of some relief—tempered by humane regrets—that I learned of the untimely fate of the individual to whom the official demand was addressed. I at once destroyed the letter which might have invalidated my claim, and pursued my inquiries in regard to the papers, the flag, the stamps, and the stools.

Through the kindness of my banker I succeeded in tracing them to the office of a Jewish ship-broker, whom I found wrapped in a bearskin coat, and smoking a very yellow meerschaum. He spoke English charmingly. He said he had succeeded (I could scarce tell how) to the late incumbent.

I asked about the suicide.

The Israelite tapped his forehead with his skinny fore-finger, waved it back and forth for a moment, and left me in a very distressing state of perplexity.

I asked after the flag, the sign-board, the table, etc. He said they were deposited in his garret, and should be delivered up whenever

I desired. He informed me further that he
knew of my appointment through a paragraph
in *Galignani's Messenger*. It seemed an odd
way of establishing my claim, to be sure; but
from the experience I had already found with
my passport, I thought it was not worth while
to shake the Jewish gentleman's belief by referring him to that instrument.

I borrowed the ship-broker's seal—the consular seal—and addressed a note to the chief
authority of the port (in obedience to home
instructions), informing him of my appointment. I furthermore addressed a large letter
to the "Department," acquainting them with
my safe arrival, and with the sad bereavement
of the State in the loss of the late acting Consul. (I learned afterward that he had been
a small ship-broker, of Hebrew extraction,
and suspected of insanity.)

The governor of the port replied to me after
a few days, informing me, courteously, that
whenever the Central Government should be
pleased to recognize my appointment, he
would acquaint me with that fact.

My next object was to find lodgings; and
as the instructions enjoined attendance from
ten until four, it was desirable that the office
should be an agreeable one, and, if possible,
contiguous to sleeping quarters.

The old Jewish gentleman, indeed, kindly offered to relieve me of all the embarrassments of the business; but I showed him a copy of the new instructions, which would not admit of my taking into employ any other than a naturalized citizen. I thought he seemed amused at this; he certainly twisted his tongue within his cheek in a very peculiar manner. Still he was courteous.

I succeeded at length in finding very airy quarters, with a large office—connected with the sleeping apartment by a garden. A bell-rope was attached to the office door, and the bell being upon the exterior wall, within the garden, could be distinctly heard throughout the apartment. This arrangement proved a very convenient one. As only three or four American ships were understood to arrive in the course of the year, and as the offiee was damp and mouldy—being just upon the water's side—I did not think it necessary (viewing the bell) to remain there constantly from ten until four. I sincerely hope that the latitude which I took in this respect will be looked on favorably by the Home Government. Indeed, considering the frequent travel of my fellow-diplomats the past season, I think I may without exaggeration presume upon indulgence.

I remained quietly one or two weeks waiting for recognition. Occasionally I walked down by the outer harbor to enjoy the sight of an American bark which just then happened to be in port, and whose commander I had the honor of meeting at the office of the Jewish ship-broker.

After six weeks of comparative quietude—broken only by mailing an occasional large letter[1] to the Department—I assumed, under official sanction, the bold step of taking possession of the seals, the papers, the stools, the flag, and the arms. They were conveyed to me, on the twelfth of the month, in a boat. I shall not soon forget the occasion. The sun shone brightly. The "arms" filled up the bow of the skiff; the papers, the stools, and the flag, were lying in the stern-sheets. I felt a glow at sight of the flag, though it was small and somewhat torn. If the office should prove lucrative, I determined to buy another at my own cost. The sign-board, or "arms," was large—larger than any I had yet seen in

[1] It should be mentioned that Government now generously assumes cost of all paper, wax, ink and steel pens consumed in the consular service. I believe the consular system is indebted for this to the liberal administrative capacity of Mr. Edward Everett, late of the State Department.

the place; much larger than the Imperial arms over the Governor's doors. I should say it must have been six feet long by four broad. The eagle was grand, and soared upon a blue sky; the olive branch, in imitation of nature, was green; the darts of a lively red.

And yet, I must admit, it seemed to me out of all proportion to the flag and to the shipping. I thought it must have been ordered by a sanguine man. It reminded me of what I had heard of the United States arms, erected in the Crystal Palace of London. I feared it was too large for the business. I never liked, I must confess, that sort of disproportion. If I might use a figurative expression,—I should say that I had never a great fancy for those fowls which crow loudly, but never lay any eggs.

If the "arms" had been of ordinary size, I should have raised it upon my roof. My serving man was anxious to do so. But I reflected that only one American ship was then in port; that it was quite uncertain when another would arrive. I reflected that the offiee-furniture was inconsiderable; even one of the stools alluded to in the official list brought to my notice at Washington, had disappeared; and instead of nine blank passports there were now only seven. I therefore retained the sign in my office, though it filled up valuable space there. I gave a formal receipt for the flag, the stamps, the arms, the stool, the table, the record books, and for a considerable budget of old papers in a very tattered condition.

Two days after, I received a bill from the late Jewish incumbent to the amount of twenty-five dollars, for repairs to flag and "arms." Having already given a receipt for the same, and communicated intelligence thereof to the seat of government, I felt reluctantly compelled to decline payment; I proposed, however, to forward the bill to the Department with all the necessary vouchers. The Jewish broker finding the matter was assuming this serious aspect, told me that the fee was a usual one on a change of consulate; and assured me jocularly, that as the consulate was changed on an average every eighteen months, the sign-board was the most profitable part of the business. I observed, indeed, that the paint was very thick upon it; and it appeared to have been spliced on one or two occasions.

There arrived, not long after, to my address, by the way of the Marseilles steamer, a somewhat bulky package. I conjectured that it contained a few knick-knacks, which I had requested a friend to forward to me from a home port. By dint of a heavy bribe to the customs men, added to the usual port charges, I succeeded in securing its delivery without delay. It proved to be a set of the United States Statutes at Large, heavily bound in law calf. A United States eagle was deeply branded upon the backs of the volumes. There was evidently a distrust of the consular character. The thought of this, in connection with the late suicide, affected me painfully. I thought—looking upon the effects around me—that I should not like to be reduced so far as to rob my consulate!

I found many hours of amusement in looking over the records of the office; they were very brief, especially in the letter department. And on comparing the condition of the records with my consular instructions, I was struck with an extraordinary discrepancy. The law, for instance, enjoined copies to be made of all letters dispatched from the office; but with the exception of three or four, dated some fifteen years back, I could not find that any had been entered. Indeed, one of my predecessors had taken a very short, and as it seemed to me, a very ingenious method of recording correspondence—in this way:

"*April* 1. Wrote Department, informing them of arrival.

"*June* 5. Wrote the Governor.

"*June* 7. Received reply from the Governor, saying he had got my letter.

"*June* 9. Wrote the Governor, blowing up the postoffice people for breaking open my letters.

"*July.* Wrote home for leave of absence, and quit the office."

I think it was about a week after the instalment of the flag and arms in my office, that I received a very voluminous packet from a native of the port, who gave me a great many titles, and informed me in the language of the country (in exceedingly fine writing), that he was the discoverer of a tremendous explosive machine, calculated to destroy fleets at a great distance, and to put an end to all marine warfare. He intimated that he was possessed of republican feelings, and would dispose of his discovery to the United States —for a consideration. After a few days— during which I had accomplished the perusal —he called for my reply.

I asked, perhaps from impertinent curiosity, if he had made any overtures to his own government?

He said he had.

I asked, with what success?

He said they had treated him with indignity, and from the explanatory gestures he made use of to confirm this statement, I have no doubt they did.

He said that genius must look for lucrative patronage beyond the ocean, and glanced wistfully at the "arms." I told him—turning my own regard in the same direction—that the United States Government was certainly a very rich and powerful one. But, I added— it was not in the habit of paying away large sums[1] of money even to native genius; not even, I continued sportively, to consular genius. I told him, if he would draw up a plan and model of his machine, I should be happy to inclose it in my budget of dispatches, for the consideration of the distinguished gentleman at the head of the Navy Department.

He asked me if I would add a strong opinion in its favor?

---

[1] This record, dating ten years back, must not be understood to impugn the economy of the present administration—whose disbursements may safely be regarded as— liberal.

I told him that I had not long been connected with the shipping interests of my country, and was hardly capable of forming an opinion about the merits of the marine machine he was good enough to bring under my notice. I was compelled further to observe, that I did not think a very high estimate was placed by government upon consular opinions of any sort. The poor man seemed satisfied—looked wistfully again at the "arms" as if they implied very extensive protection—bade me good morning and withdrew.

The weeks wore on, and there was no American arrival; nor did I hear anything of my recognition by the Central Government. I drew up in a careful manner, two new record books in obedience to law, and transcribed therein my various notes to the department and foreign personages, in a manner that I am sure was utterly unprecedented in the annals of the office. I prepared the blank of a passport for signature—in case one should be needed—thus reducing the effective number of those instruments to six. I even drew up the blank of a bill against Captain *Blank* (to be filled up on arrival) for *blank* charges. Most of my charges, indeed, may be said to have been *blank* charges.

On one occasion, about three weeks after full possession of the "effects," there was a violent ring at the office bell. I hurried down with my record books and inkstand, which I had transferred for security to my sleeping quarters. It proved, however, to be a false alarm: it was a servant who had rung at the wrong door. He asked my pardon in a courteous manner, and went away. I replaced the record books in the office drawer, and retired to my apartment.

I think it was some two or three days after this, when I heard of a large ship standing "off and on" at the mouth of the harbor. I was encouraged to think, by a friendly party, that she might be an American vessel. I even went upon the tower of the town to have a look at her with my spy-glass (a private spy-glass). There was no flag flying; and she was too far off to make her out by the rig. She came up, however, the next day, and proved to be a British bark from Newcastle.

Matters were in this condition, the office wearing its usual quiet air, when I was waited on one morning by a weazen-faced little gentleman, who spoke English with pertinacity, and a slight accent. He informed me that he had been at one period incumbent of the office which I now held. He asked, in a kind manner, after the Government?

I thanked him, and told him that by last advices they were all very well.

He said that he was familiar with the details of the consular business, and would be happy to be of service to me.

I thanked him in the kindest manner; but assured him that the business was not yet of so pressing a character as to demand an assistant. (Indeed, with the exception of four or five letters dispatched in various directions, and the preparation of the blanks already alluded to, I had, in the course of two or three months, performed no important consular act whatever.) My visitor diverted consideration as gracefully as his English would allow, to the climate and the society of the port. He said he should be happy to be of service to me in a social way; and alluded to one or two government balls which, on different occasions, he had the honor of attending in a consular capacity. I thanked him again, without, however, preferring any very special request.

After musing a moment, he resumed conversation by asking me "if I had a coat?"

I did not fully understand him at first; and replied at a venture, that I had several.

"Very true," said he, "but have you the buttons?"

I saw that he alluded to the official costume, and told him that I had not. Whereupon he said that he had only worn his coat upon one or two occasions; and he thought that, with a slight alteration, it would suit admirably my figure.

I thanked him again; but taking from the drawer the thin copy of consular instructions, I read to him those portions which regarded the new order respecting plain clothes. I told him, in short, that the blue and the gilt (for I had not then heard of the re-introduction of the dress system in various European capitals) had utterly gone by. He seemed disappointed; but presently recovered animation, and remarked that he had in his possession a large American flag, which he had purchased while holding the consular office, and which (as the Government had declined paying for the same), he would be happy to sell to me at a great reduction on the original cost.

I told him that the affairs of the consulate were still in an unsettled state; but in the event of business turning out well, I thought that the Government might be induced to enter into negotiations for the purchase. (I had my private doubts of this, however.)

At my mention of the Government again, he seemed disheartened. He soon asked me, in his broken manner (I think he was of Dutch origin), "If the Gouverman vass not a ittle mean about tose tings?"

I coughed at this; very much as the stationer, Mr. Snagsby, used to cough when he made an observation in Mrs. Snagsby's presence. But, collecting myself, I said that the Government had shown great liberality in the sign-board, and doubted if a larger one was to be found in Europe. He surprised me, however, by informing me in a prompt manner, that he had expended a pound sterling upon it, out of his own pocket!

I hoped, mildly, that he had been reimbursed. He replied, smartly, that he had not been. He continued courteous, however; and would, I think, upon proper representations on the part of the Government, be willing to resume negotiations.

A fortnight more succeeded, during which several bills came in—for the record books, postage, hire of an office-boat, rent of office, beside some repairs I had ordered to the office table. I had even gone so far as to buy a few bottles of old wine, and a package of Havana cigars, for the entertainment of any friendly captains who might arrive. Affairs were in this condition when I heard, one morning, upon the public square of the town, that an American vessel had been seen some miles down the gulf, and it was thought that she might bear up for this harbor. I went home to my rooms in a state of excitement it is quite impossible to describe. I dusted the record books, and rubbed up the backs of the United States Statutes at Large. (I should have mentioned that I had added my private copy of Vattel to the consular library; together, they really made an imposing appearance.)

I took the precaution of oiling the pulley to the office bell. My servant-man had hinted that it *had* sometimes failed to ring. I ordered him to give it repeated trials, while I took up a position in my apartment. It rang distinctly, and so vigorously that I feared the occupants of the adjoining house might be disturbed. I therefore approached the window, and giving a concerted signal, ordered my serving-man to abstain.

He was evidently in high spirits at the good order in which matters stood. He renewed his proposal to place the sign-board upon the roof of the house. I found, however, upon inquiry, that it would involve the labor of three men for half a day; I therefore abandoned the idea. I authorized him, however, to apply a fresh coating of varnish, and to place it in a conspicuous position upon the side of the office fronting the door.

He wiped his forehead, and said it was a *"disegnetto meraviglioso"*—a wonderful little design!

The wind continued for some days northerly, and no vessel came into port. On the fourth day, however, I received a note from a friendly party, stating that an American bark had arrived. I gave a dollar to the messenger who brought the news. I saw the intelligence confirmed in the evening journal. I was in great trepidation all the following day. At length, a little after the town clock had struck twelve, the captain came. I hurried into the office to meet him. He was a tall, blear-eyed man, in a damaged black beaver with a narrow rim, tight-sleeved black dress-coat, and cowhide boots.

I greeted him warmly, and asked him how he was?

He thanked me, and said he was "pretty

smart." I regretted that I had not some rum-and-water. The old wine I did not think he would appreciate. In short, I was disappointed in my countryman. I should not like to have sailed with him, much less to have served under him. Before leaving the offiee, he cautioned me against a sailor who might possibly come to me with his "cussed" complaints: he said he was an "ugly devil," and I had best have nothing to do with him.

True enough, the next morning a poor fellow presented himself, speaking very broken English, and complaining that he was sadly abused—showing, indeed, a black eye, and a lip frightfully bloated. I ordered my serving-man to prepare him a little breakfast. This was not, perhaps, a legitimate consular attention, but it proved a grateful one; and the man consumed two or three slices of broiled ham with extraordinary relish. After this he told me a long story of the abuses he had undergone, and of his desire to get a discharge. I asked him if he had an American protection? He said he had bought one upon the dock in New York, shortly before sailing, and had paid a half eagle for it, but it was lost.

This was unfortunate; and upon referring to the ship's crew list, I found that the cus-

toms' clerk had dispatched the whole subject
of nationalities in a very summary manner.
He had written the words "U. States" up and
down the sheet in such an affluent style as to
cover two-thirds, or three-quarters or, (reckoning the flourishes of his capitals) even the
whole body of the crew. Now as some four
or five of them were notoriously, and avow-
edly, as foreign as foreign birth, language
and residence could make them, I was compelled to think lightly of the authority of the
customs' clerk.

The Consular Instructions, moreover, I
found were not very definite in regard to the
circumstance under which a discharge might
be granted. But the most trying difficulty of
all was the fact that I was not as yet—in the
eyes of the authorities—a Consul at all. Although I might discharge the poor fellow, I
could neither procure him admittance to the
hospital, or furnish him with such papers as
would be counted valid. I could, indeed, pro-
tect him under the shadow of the arms and
the flag; but should he tire of the broiled ham,
and venture an escapade, he might, for aught
that I knew, be clapped into prison as a vaga-
bond.

I stated the matter to him cautiously; alluding, with some embarrassment, to my own present lack of authority; advising him of the comparative infrequency of American vessels at that port; and counselling him, in sober earnest, to stick by the ship, if possible, until he reached an adjoining port, where he would find a recognized consul and more abundant shipping.

The consequence was, the poor fellow slunk back to his ship, and the captain assured me, in a gay humor, (I fear it was his habit to joke in such matters with brother Consuls), that he "got a good *lamming* for his pains."

When the vessel was ready to leave, I made out her papers. I doubt very much if any ship's papers were ever made out with nicer attention to formalities. I warmed up the stamp and printer's ink for some hours by a low fire, in order to secure a good impression of the consular seal. Without vanity, I may say that I succeeded. I doubt if such distinct impressions were ever before issued from that office. The bill was, I think, a model in its way; it certainly was so for its amount; for though I strained it to the full limit of the Instructions, it fell at least one-third short of the usual bills upon the record.

Upon the day of sailing (and I furnished

my serving-man with an extra bottle of wine on the occasion), I presented myself at the office of the Port Captain, with the usual vouchers respecting the ship and crew under my charge. To my great vexation, however, that gentleman politely informed me that he was not yet advised officially of my appointment—that my seal and signature in short (so elaborately done) were of no possible service.

The skipper who attended me, rubbed his hat with his elbow in a disturbed manner.

What was to be done?

The Captain of the Port suggested that he was himself empowered to act as Consul for such powers as were unrepresented; and he instanced, if I remember rightly, some of the Barbary States.

I withdrew my papers, and my charge for services which had proved so unavailing. I am afraid I was petulant to the serving-man. Thus far the Consulate had not come up to expectations. I began to distrust the value of the place. I wrote off a sheet full of expostulations to the Governor; another to the authorities at home; and a third to our representative at the Court. This last promised very strenuous exertion in my behalf; and he was as good as his word; for a week after I was gratified with a sight of my name, regularly gazetted under the "Official heading" of the daily journals of the place. The same evening the Governor of the Port addressed to me an official note, upon an immense sheet of foolscap, giving the information already conveyed to me in the Gazette.

Nor was this the end of my triumph; for the next day, or shortly afterward, a band of street performers on various instruments (chiefly, however, their lungs), came under my windows in a body, and played several gratulatory airs to my success in procuring recognition. They even followed up the music by shouting in a most exhilarating manner. It showed kind-feeling; and I was just observing to myself the hospitable interest of these people, when my serving-man entered in great glee, and informed me that it was usual on these occasions to pay a small fee to the performers.

I can hardly say I was surprised at this; I asked—how much? He said he would count them, and thought about three shillings apiece (our money[1]) would be sufficient. As there

[1] I mean by this, of the value of our Government money; and not, literally, Government money; of which, indeed, I saw very little—very.

113

were but fifteen, I did not think it high. I wondered if it had been the habit to charge this matter in the stationery account?

The day after (for now I seemed to be growing rapidly in importance), I received a very bulky package from the chief of police, inclosing the passport, unpaid bills, subscription papers, recommendations, and police descriptions of one David Humfries, who, I was informed, was in the port prison, for various misdemeanors—chiefly for vagabondage; and who, being an American citizen, was at my disposal. The chief of police expressed a wish that I would take charge of the same, and put him out of the country.

I examined the papers. They were curious. He appeared to have figured in a variety of characters. An Italian subscription list represented him as the father of a needy family. A German one of about the same date, expressed a desire that charitable people would assist a stranger in returning to his home and friends at the Cape of Good Hope. Among the bills was a rather long one for beer and brandy.

I thought it would be patriotic to call upon my countryman. I therefore left a note "absent on business," in the office window, and called at the prison. I was ushered, under the charge of an official, into a dingy, grated room upon the second floor, and was presented to a stout negro-man, who met me with great self-possession,—apologized for his dress (which indeed was somewhat scanty), and assured me that he was not the man he seemed.

I found him indeed possessed of somewhat rare accomplishments, speaking German and French with very much the same facility as English. He informed me that he was a native of the Cape of Good Hope, though a naturalized citizen of the country I represented. His passport was certainly perfectly in order, and signed by a late Chargé, Mr. Foote of Vienna. He assured me farther, that he was of excellent family; and that his father was a respectable man, well known in New York, and the head of a large school in that city. I told him of the application of the police, and of their wish to be rid of him.

He did not appear to manifest resentment; but said he would consent to any reasonable arrangement. He had no objection to go to New York, provided his wardrobe were put in a proper condition. He should be sorry, he said, to meet the old gentleman (meaning the schoolmaster) in his present guise.

I told him I was sorry that the law did not

warrant me in finding him a wardrobe, and that only by a fiction could I class him among seamen, and provide him with a passage home. Upon this, he avowed himself (in calm weather) a capital sailor, and said he had once served as cook.

I accordingly wrote to the authorities, engaging to ship him by the first American vessel which should touch the port. By rare accident this happened a fortnight after; and having given a receipt for the black man, besides supplying him with a few flannel shirts at my own cost, I succeeded in placing him on board a home-bound ship, by giving the captain an order on the Treasury for ten dollars; the captain intimating, meantime, that "he would get thirty dollars' worth of work out of him, or take off his black skin."

I did not envy the black man his voyage: I have not had the pleasure of hearing from Mr. Humfries since that date.

I have spoken of the arrival of a second American ship; such was the fact. I need not say that the papers were made out in the same style as the previous ones; I had now gained considerable facility in the use of the seal. Upon the payment of the fees I ventured to attach the seal to my receipt for the same. It was not necessary—it was not usual even; still I did it. If the occasion were to be renewed, I think I should do it again.

Not long after this accession of business, which gave me considerable hopes of—in time —replacing the flag, I received a visit from an Italian gentleman just arrived from New York, where he had been an attaché to an opera troupe. He informed me with some trepidation that the authorities were not satisfied with his papers, and had given him notice to return by sea.

I asked him if he was an American: whereupon he showed me a court certificate of his intentions to become a citizen, dated a couple of days before his leave, and with it an imposing-looking paper, illustrated by a stupendous eagle. This last, however, I found upon examination, was only the instrument of an ambitious Notary Public, who testified, thereby, to the genuine character of the court certificate, and at the same time invited all foreign powers to treat the man becomingly. The paper, indeed, had very much the air of a passport, and, by the Italian's account, had cost a good deal more.

I told him I should be happy to do what I could for him, and would cheerfully add my testimony to the *bona fide* character of the court certificate.

The man, however, wished a passport.

I told him that the only form of passport of which I knew (and I showed the six blanks), involved a solemn declaration on my part, that the party named was an American citizen. The Italian gentleman alluded to M. Koszta and the New-York Herald.

I expressed an interest in both; but told him that I had as yet no knowledge of the correspondence in the Koszta affair; that there had been no change in the consular instructions (and I showed him the little pamphlet).

I promised, however, to communicate with the Chargé, who might be in possession of later advices; and, in addition, offered to intercede with the authorities to grant permission to an unoffending gentleman to visit his friends in the country.

Upon this I undertook a considerable series of notes and letters,—by far the most elaborate and numerous which had yet issued from my consular bureau. I will not presume to say how many there were, or how many visits I paid to the lodging-quarters of the suspected gentleman. I found it requisite,—to secure him any freedom of action,—to become sponsor for his good conduct. I need not say (after this) that I felt great solicitude about him.

The notice of "absent on business" became almost a fixture in the office window. I had written previously to the Department for instructions in the event of such application; I had never received them; indeed I never did. The Chargé flatteringly confirmed my action, and "relied on my discretion." I was sorry to find he relied so much upon it.

It seemed to me that an office involving so large discretion should, at the least, have better furniture. The stool, though now repaired, was a small stool. I sat upon it nervously. The "Statutes at Large" I looked on with pride and satisfaction. I had inaugurated them so to speak, in the office. I placed my little Vattel by the side of them; I hope it is there now—though there was no eagle on the back.

To return to the Italian gentleman, I at length succeeded in giving him a safe clearance. I think he was grateful: he certainly wore a grateful air when he left my office for the last time, and I felt rewarded for my labor. It was the only reward, indeed, I received: if he had offered a fee, I *think* I should have declined. Was I not there, indeed, for the service of my countrymen, and of my intended countrymen? Of course I was.

The day after the Italian gentleman left I paid my office rent for the current month, besides a small bill the serving-man brought me for the caulking of the office boat. It appeared that it had grounded with the tide, and without our knowledge (there being no American ships in port), had remained exposed for several days to the sun.

Keeping the office in business trim, and sitting upon the office stool, I received, one day, a very large packet, under the seal of the Department. I had not heard from Washington in a long time, and it was a pleasant surprise to me. Possibly it might be some new and valuable commission; possibly, it might bring the details of the proposed change in the Consular system. Who knew?

In such an event I wondered what the probable salary would be at my post; something handsome, no doubt. I glanced at the "arms" of my country with pride, and (there being no American ship in port), broke open the packet.

It contained two circulars, embracing a series of questions, ninety in number, in regard to ship-building, ship-timber, rigging, hemp, steamships, fuel, provisioning of vessels, light-house dues, expenses of harbor, depth of ditto, good anchorages, currents, winds, cutting of channels, buoys, rates of wages, apprentices, stowage facilities, prices current, duties, pro-tests, officers of port, manufactures, trade fa-cilities, leakages, wear and tear, languages, pilots, book publication, etc., etc., on all of which points the circulars requested full infor-mation, as soon as practicable, in a tabular form, with a list of such works as were pub-lished on kindred subjects, together with all Government orders in regard to any, or all of the suggested subjects, which were in pamphlet form; and if in a foreign language, the same to be accurately translated into American.

The accompanying letter stated that it was proposed to allow no remuneration for the same; but added, "faithful acquittal of the proposed task will be favorably viewed."

I reflected—(I sometimes do reflect).

A respectable reply even to the questions suggested, would, supposing every facility was thrown in my way by port officers and others, involve the labor of at least six weeks, and the writing over of at least ninety large pages of foolscap paper (upon which it was requested that the report should be made).

I reflected, farther—that the port officer, as yet affecting a large share of his old ignorance, would, upon presentation of even the first inquiries as to the depth of the harbor, send me to the guard-house as a suspicious person; or, recognizing my capacity, would report the question as a diplomatic one to the Governor; who would report it back to the Central Cabinet; who would report it back to the maritime commander in an adjoining city; who would communicate on the subject with the police of the port; who would communicate back with the marine intendant; who would report accordingly to the Central Government; who would in due time acquaint the Chargé at the capital with their conclusions.

I reflected—that I had already expended, on behalf of the Government, more of time and of money than I should probably (there being no American ship in port) ever receive again at their hands.

I reflected—that life was, so to speak, limited; and that in case I should determine to give it up to gratuitous work for my country, or, indeed, for any party whatever,—I should prefer that the object of my charity should be a needy object.

I reflected—that I had given bonds in the

sum of two thousand dollars (with sound bondsmen) for the stool, the blank passports, the pewter and brass seals, the small-sized flag, and the "arms;" and I examined them with attention.

I reflected—that while these things were in a capital state of preservation, and my health still unimpaired, I had better withdraw from office.

I therefore sent in my resignation.

I do not think there has been any omission in the performance of my consular duties; it involved, indeed, a more expensive charity on my part than I am in the habit of extending to the indigent. I trust that the Government is grateful.

In overlooking my books I find charges against the Government for nineteen dollars and sixty-three cents for postages and stationery. To make the sum an even one I have drawn on the Government (after the form prescribed in the consular instructions) for twenty dollars, making an over-draft of thirty-seven cents, for which I hope the Government will take into consideration my office and boat rent, my time and repairs to the consular stool.

Finding the draft difficult of negotiation upon the great European exchanges, I may add that I have carried it for a long time in my pocket. Should it be eventually paid, I shall find myself in possession,—by adding the thirty-seven cents to sums received in fees during the period of my consulate,—of the amount of some thirty dollars, more or less.

I have not yet determined how to invest this. I am hoping that Mr. Powers, who I hear wears the title of Consul, will find some pretty Florentine model-woman to make an "America" of. If he does so, and will sell a small plaster cast at a reasonable price, I will buy it with my consular income, and install the figure (if not too nude) in my study, as a consular monument.

I shall be happy to welcome my successor; I will give him all the aid in my power; I will present him to the ten-penny reading-room, and shall be happy to inscribe his name in advance at either of the hotels. I will inform him of the usual anchorage ground of American ships, so far as my observation has gone. I shall be pleased to point out to him, through the indulgence of my serving-man, the best grocer's shop in the port, and another where are sold wines and varnish.

Should the office-stool require repair, I think I could recommend with confidence a small journeyman joiner in a neighboring court.

He will have my best hopes for lucrative employment in his new position, and for happiness generally.

For myself, consular recollections are not, I regret to say, pleasant. I do not write "Ex-United States Consul" after my name. I doubt if I ever shall.

All my disturbed dreams at present take a consular form. I waked out of a horrid nightmare only a few nights since, in which I fancied that I was bobbing about fearfully in a boat—crashing against piles and door-posts—waiting vainly for an American captain.

I have no objection to serve my country; I have sometimes thought of enlisting in the dragoons. I am told they have comfortable rations, and two suits of clothes in a year. But I pray Heaven that I may never again be deluded into the acceptance of a small consulate on the Mediterranean.

POSTSCRIPT

THE foregoing story of a Consulate was written in the year 1854, and by a singular mishap, which gave the seal to my marine misfortunes, the first draft of it went down in the ill-fated steamer Arctic. In the following year, however, it was re-written, and given to the public in the columns of Harper's Magazine.

Since that date, I am happy to say that our Foreign Consulates have been placed upon a more dignified footing. Every man who represents the government abroad is insured at least so much of stipend, as to enable him to caulk his own boat, and to wear his own coat. It is to be hoped that under the new dispensation, the consular business, at the port alluded to, is progressing swimmingly. Indeed, the natural features of the port—which, without impropriety, I may name as Venice—strongly encourage this belief.

With unimportant exceptions, I have never held official position since that day. I have indeed served as one of five vestry-men in a small church of ten male members; but it being thought desirable to rotate, so as to give a kind of official dignity to all the congregation, I count at the present writing,—simply as pew-holder. I was also (if the reader will excuse the egotism) at one time a director in a thriving Horticultural Society: but after a series of errors in the adjustment of the qualities of different fruits, and a shocking display of ignorance in respect to the merits of certain new seeds sent out by the Patent Office, I was —to use the amiable expression—retired from the direction. The place is now held, I believe, by a gentleman who courageously plants and eats the Dioscorea Batata. Such a man deserves reward; and if it did not come in the way of official honor, I hardly know in what way it could come.

THIRD STORY

THE PETIT SOULIER

THIRD STORY

THE PETIT SOULIER

My old friend the Abbé G——, who on my earliest visit to Paris, not only taught me French, but put me in the way of a great deal of familiar talk-practice with his pleasant bourgeois friends, lived in a certain dark corner of a hotel in the Rue de Seine, or in the Rue de la Harpe; which of the two it was I really forget. At any rate, the hotel was very old, and the street out of which I used to step into its ill-paved triangular court was very narrow, and very dirty.

At the end of the court, farthest from the entrance-way, was the box of the *concierge*, who was a brisk little shoe-maker, forever bethwacking his lap-stone. If I remember rightly, the hammer of this little *cordonnier* made the only sound that broke the stillness within; for though the hotel was full of lodgers, I think I never saw two of them together;

and it is quite certain, that even in mid-summer, no voices were ever to be heard talking across the court.

At this distance of time, I do not think it would be possible for me to describe accurately all the windings of the corridor which led to the Abbé's door. I remember that the first part was damp and low—that after **it,** came a sweaty old stairway of stone; and once arrived at the top of this, I used to traverse an open-sided gallery which looked down upon a quiet interior court; then came a little wooden wicket, dank with long handling— which when it opened tinkled a bell. Sometimes the Abbé would hear the bell, and open his door, down at the end of some farther passage; and sometimes a lodger, occupying a room that looked upon the last mentioned court, would draw slyly a corner of his curtain, and peep out to see who might be passing. Occasionally I would amuse myself by giving to the little warning bell an unnecessary tinkle, in order that I might study some of the faces which should peer out from the lodgments upon the court; yet I saw very little to gratify me; and upon the damp flagging which covered the area of the court, I rarely saw any one moving; at most, only a decrepit old woman shuffling along with broom in hand; or a boy, in paper cap, from some neighboring shop, whistling an air he may have caught from the orchestra at the Odeon, and disappearing through a dilapidated door-way —the only one to be seen.

It appeared to me a quarter, that with its quaint, old-fashioned windows, piling story above story, and its oppressive quietude, ought to show some face or figure that should pique curiosity, and so relieve the dulness of my lessons with the good Abbé. 'But all the faces that met my eye were the most matter of fact in the world.

From time to time, as we passed out through the open-sided corridor, I would draw the Abbé's attention to the silent court, and ask— who lived in the little room at the top?

"Ah, *mon cher*, I do not know."

Or, "who lives in the corner, with the narrow loop-hole, and the striped curtain?"

"I can not tell you, *mon cher*."

"And whose is the little window with so many broken panes, and an old placard pinned against the sash?"

"Ah, who knows? perhaps a rag-picker, or a shopman or perhaps"——and the Abbé lifted his finger, shaking his head expressively—"It is a strange world we live in, *mon ami.*"

What could the Abbé mean? I looked up at the window again: it was small, and the glass was set in rough metal casing: it must have been upon the fourth or the fifth floor; but there was nothing to be seen within, save the dirty yellow placard.

"Is it in the same hotel with you?" said I.

"Ma foi, I do not know."

The Abbé had unconsciously given a little foot-hold, by aid of which my imagination might climb into a good romance. The chamber must be small; indeed, there were few, even upon the first floor, in that neighborhood, which were large. Comfortless, too, no doubt; the yellow placard told me how that must be.

I cannot undertake to describe all that fancy painted to me, in connection with that window of the dreary, silent hotel. Did some miserly old scoundrel live in the chamber, who counted his hoardings night after night? Was it some apprentice boy from the provinces who had pinned up the yellow placard—more to shut out the intruding air, than the light? I even lingered very late at the Abbé's rooms, to see if I could detect by the glow of any lamp within the chamber, the figure of its occupant. But either the light was too feeble or the oceu-pants were too quiet. Week after week, as I threaded every day the corridor, I looked out at the brooding, gloomy windows, and upon the mouldy pavement of the court, hoping for a change of aspect, that would stimulate curiosity, or give some hint of the character of the lodgers. But no such change appeared: day after day, there remained the same provoking quietude; nor could I with all my art seduce the good-natured Abbé into any appetizing conjectures in regard to the character of his neighbors.

My observation at last grew very careless, and I suspect would have been abandoned al-together, if I had not one day in my casual glances about the dim court, noticed a fragment of lace hanging within the little window where we had seen the yellow placard. Rich lace it was too. My occasional study of the shop windows enabled me to give competent judgment on this score. It may have been a bridal veil;—but whose? I could hardly have believed that a bit of dainty feminine attire should on a sudden have lent such new interest to the court of this dingy old lodging house of Paris. And yet it was as if a little wood-bird straying in, had filled the whole court with a blithe song.

There are some of us who never get over listening to those songs.

I wanted to share my enthusiasm with the good Abbé—so I told him what I had seen.

"And you think there is a bride quartered there, *mon ami?*" And he shook his head: "It is more likely a broidery girl who is drudging at a bit of finery for some *magasin de luxe,* which will pay the poor girl only half the value of her work."

I could not gainsay this: "And have you seen her?" said I.

"*Mon ami,* (very seriously) I do not know if there is any such; and —*tenez—mon enfant—gardez vous bien d'en savoir plus que moi!*"

A few weeks later—it was on a winter's morning, after a light snow had fallen—I chanced to glance over into the court, upon which the window that had so piqued my curiosity looked down, and saw there the print of a lady's slipper. It was scarce larger than my hand—too delicately formed to have been left by a child's foot—least of all by the foot of such children as I saw from time to time in the neighboring hotels. I could not but associate it with the lace veil I had seen above. I felt sure that no broidery girl could leave such delicate foot-print on the snow. Even the shop-girls of the Rue de la Paix, or the tidiest Lorettes, would be crazed with envy, at sight of so dainty a slipper.

Through all the morning lesson—I was then reading *La Grammaire des Grammaires*—I could think of nothing but the pretty foot-track in the snow.

After lesson, the Abbé took his usual stroll with me; and as we traversed the corridor, I threw my eye over carelessly—as if it had been my first observation—saying, "My dear Abbé, the snow tells tales this morning."

The Abbé looked curiously down, ran his eye rapidly over the adjoining windows, shook his head expressively, and said, as he glanced down again, *"C'était un fort joli petit soulier, mon ami."*

"Whose was it?" said I.

"Ah, *mon enfant,* I do not know."

"Can any broidery girl boast such a foot?"

"Mon enfant," (with despairing manner) "how could I know?"

Such little, unimportant circumstances as I have noted, would never have occasioned remark in a court of the Rue de Rivoli: but in this mouldy quarter, which by common consent was given over to lodging-house keepers, grisettes, shopmen, sub-officials, medical students, and occasional priests, any evidences of feminine delicacy and refinement—and as such I could not forbear counting both foot-print and veil—were harshly out of place. Great misfortune, or great crime could alone drift them into so dreary a corner of the old city.

I hinted as much to the Abbé.

"Possibly," said he; "ah, *mon enfant*—if the world were only better! Great misfortunes and great crime are all around us."

I seized a sly occasion to consult the *concierge;*—were there any female lodgers in the house? The little shoe-maker—with his hammer suspended, and a merry twinkle in his eye —says, "*Oui monsieur*—the aunt of the tobacconist at the corner—*belle femme!*"

"No others?"

"*Personne.*"

And do the little windows looking upon the inner court belong to the hotel? he doubts it; if monsieur wishes, he will go see: and he lays down his hammer, and comes upon the corridor—"no; he knows nothing of them; the entrance must be two, perhaps three doors below."

From morning to morning, before my lessons begin, I loiter about the entrance to the adjoining courts; but I saw nothing to quicken my curiosity or to throw any light upon the little waifs of story which I had seen in the veil and the foot-prints. Stolid, commonplace people only, plodded in and out of the entrance gates, to which my observation was now extended; haggard old women clattering over the pavement in *sabots,* or possibly a tidily dressed shop-girl, whose figure alone would forbid any association with the delicate foot-print in the snow. I remarked indeed an elderly man in a faded military cloak muffled closely about him, passing out on one or two occasions from the third court below the hotel of the Abbé: his figure and gait were certainly totally unlike the habitués of the quarter; but his presence there, even though connected with the little window of the dreary court, would only add to the mystery of the foot-print and of the lace.

It happened upon a certain morning, not long after, as I paced through the open corridor, and threw a glance up at the loop-hole upon which I had chosen to fasten my freak of observation that I saw a slight change: a muslin handkerchief was stetched across the window, within the placard, (I could plainly see its embroidered border,) and while I stood regarding it, a delicate pair of hands (the taper fingers I saw plainly) removed the fastenings, and presently this other token of feminine presence was gone.

I told the Abbé of my observation.

He closed his book, "La Grammaire des Grammaires"—(keeping his thumb at the place of our lesson) and gave me, I dare say, an admirable little lecture,—which certainly was not in the grammar. I know the French was good; I believe the sentiment was good; but all the while of its delivery, my imagination was busy in conjuring into form some charming neighbor of whom I had only seen the delicate, frail fingers, and the wonderful foot-print on the snow.

When he had finished the lecture, we accomplished the lesson.

My next adventure in the way of discovery was with the little *concierge,* who presided over the court where I had seen the tall gentleman of the military cloak, pass in. He was quietly dipping his roll in a bowl of coffee, when I commenced my inquiries.

"Were there any rooms in the hotel to be let?" Not that I desired to change from my

THE PETIT SOULIER

comfortable quarters over the river; but it seemed to me the happiest method of conciliating a communicative temper.

"Oui, Monsieur," responds the brisk *concierge,* as he gives his roll a dip upon the edge of his coffee bowl, and with a cheering, heavy bite—takes down a key here, and a key there, until he is provided for all the rooms at his disposition. We mount together damp stone stair-ways and enter upon apartments with glazed tile floors; we mount higher to waxed, oaken parqueterie; but I like the full glow of the sun; we must go higher. Upon the fourth floor, there is a vacant room; its solitary window has a striped red curtain, and it looks out —as I suspected—upon the court of the open corridor, where I had so long carried on my furtive observations. The window which had particularly arrested my attention, must be just above.

"Was there no room still higher?"

"Parbleu, il y en a une; monsieur ne se fâche pas de monter, donc?"

No, I love the air and the sunshine. But the little room into which he shows me looks into a strange court I do not know; I bustle out, and toward the opposite door.

"Pardon, monsieur; it is occupied."

141

And even as he speaks, the door opens; an old white haired gentleman, the very one I have seen in the military cloak looks out, disturbed; and (I think it is not a fancy) there is the whisk of a silk dress moving within.

The concierge makes his apologies, and we go below.

"Will the chamber occupied by the old gentleman be vacant soon?"

"It is possible," but he cannot truly say.

Farther down the stairs we encountered the wife of the concierge, at her work. He appeals to her: "Does Monsieur Verier leave soon?"

She cannot say. The marriage is off; and he may stay.

It gives me a hint for further inquiry.

"Est-ce que ce vieux va se marier, donc?"

"Pardon, monsieur; but he has a daughter. *Ah, qu'elle est gentille!* (and the concierge looks upward reverently). There was a marriage arranged, and the old gentleman was to live with the daughter. But as my wife says—it 's off now: the old man has his humors." ,

So at last the bridal veil was explained.

"But does the daughter lodge here with the father?" said I.

"Ah, no, monsieur; impossible: a chamber at fifty francs too! It 's very droll; and the daughter drives in a grand coach to the door; but it 's not often; and my wife who showed her the chamber tells me that their first meeting—and it was after the old gentleman had been here a month or more—was as if they had not met in years. She comes mostly of an evening or early morning, when few are stirring, as if she were afraid to be seen, and she is veiled and muffled in a shawl too—*cependant elle est gentille. Tenez,*" said he, pointing to a charming little lithographic head of St. Agnes, in his *conciergerie* (which we had now reached) *"voici sa tête!"*

"And has she no attendant upon her visits?"

"*Ma foi,* I cannot tell you: once or twice a gentleman has descended from the carriage into the court, as if to watch for her—but who it may have been I know no more than you. To tell you the truth, monsieur, I have my doubts of the old gentleman's story about the coming marriage: he has a feeble head, and talks wildly of his daughter. I can make nothing of it. I can make nothing of her either,—except that she has the face of an angel."

"Not a fallen one, I hope." And I said it more for the sake of giving a turn to a French phrase, than with any seriousness. (In this light way we banter with character!)

"*Parbleu!*" says the concierge indignantly, "*on ne peut pas s'y tromper:* she is as pure as the snow."

I had now a full budget of information to lay before the Abbé, and trusted to his good nature to give me some interpretation of this bit of history which was evolving under his very wing. Yet the Abbé was lost; as much lost as I. But I was glad to perceive that I had succeeded in kindling in him a little interest in regard to his neighbor; and the next morning, as we strolled through the corridor, I think he looked up at the window, where the yellow placard was hanging, with as much curiosity as ever I had done.

A few days after, I was compelled to leave suddenly for the South; but I counselled the good Abbé to be constant at my old watch, and to have a story to tell me on my return.

II

TEN months passed before I came to Paris again; and it was not until three days after my return, that I found my way to the familiar old corridor that led to the Abbé's room, and caught myself scanning once more the aspect of the dingy court. The yellow placard **was** gone; the little window was, if possible, still more dilapidated, and an adventurous spider had hung his filmy web across all the broken panes. The Abbé was in his soutane, and had just returned from attendance upon the funeral service at the grave of a friend. A few stout gentlemen from the provinces were present in the Abbé's rooms, who were near relatives of the dead man; and though the good old priest's look was all it should have been, I cannot say as much for the buxom family mourners; grief never appears to me to mate well with too much stoutness: its sharp edge cannot reveal itself, with any cutting appeal, in a rubicund visage, and a rotund figure. I fear that I do a great many heavy people injustice; for there are brave, good hearts hid under great weight of flesh; yet I think the reflection finds justification in a certain poetic law of proprieties, and a fat undertaker or a fat hearse-man would be a very odious thing.

When I left the Abbé's rooms, I walked down the street, thinking I would call upon my old friend the concierge of the third door below, and inquire after Monsieur Verier: but I had no sooner reached the open court, than I turned at once upon my heel, and strolled away.

I was fairly afraid to inquire; I would toy with my little romance a while longer; perhaps, on the very afternoon I might meet the old gentleman rejuvenated, or sharing the carriage of the charming St. Agnes upon the Boulevards. At farthest, I knew that to-morrow the Abbé would have something to tell me of his life.

And this proved true. We dined together next day at Vefour's in the Palais Royal—a quiet dinner, in a little cabinet above stairs.

The soup was gone, and an appetizing dish of *éperlans* was before us—the Abbé in his old fashioned way had murmured—"*vôtre santé*" —over a delectable glass of Chambertin,— before I ventured to ask one word about Monsieur Verier.

"Ah, *mon cher,*" said the Abbé, at the same time laying down his fork—"he is dead!"

"And *mademoiselle?*"

"*Attendez,*" said the Abbé, "and you shall hear it all."

I refilled the glasses; and as we went on leisurely with the dinner, he leisurely went on with his narrative.

"You will remember, *mon ami,* having described to me the person of the tall gentleman who was my neighbor. The description was a good one, for I recognized him the moment I saw him.

"It was a week or more after you had left for the South, and I had half forgotten—excuse me, *mon enfant,*—the curiosity you had felt about the little foot-print in the court, when I happened to be a half hour later than usual in returning from morning mass, and as I passed the hotel of which you had spoken, I saw coming out, a gentleman wrapped in a military cloak, and with an air so unlike that of most lodgers of the quarter, that I knew him in a moment for your friend Monsieur Verier."

"The very same," said I.

"Indeed," continued the Abbé, "I was so struck with his appearance—added to your interest in him—(here the Abbé bowed and sipped his wine) that I determined to follow him a short way down the street. We kept through the Rue de Seine, and passing under the colonnade of the Institute, crossed the *Pont de Fer,* continued along the Quay, as far as the gates of the garden, crossed the garden into the Rue de Rivoli, and though I thought he would have stopped at some of the cafés in the neighborhood, he did not, but kept steadily on, nor did I give up pursuit, until he had taken his place in one of the omnibuses which pass the head of the Rue de la Paix.

"A week after, happening to see him again, as I came from Martin's under the Odeon, I followed him a second time. At the head of the Rue de la Paix I took a place in the same omnibus. He left the stage opposite the Rue de Lancry. I stopped a short distance above, and stepping back, soon came up with the poor gentleman picking his feeble way along the dirty *trottoir*.

"You remember, my friend, wandering with me in the Rue de Lancry; you remember that it is crooked and long. The poor gentleman found it so; and before he had reached the end, I saw that he was taking breath, and such rest as he might, upon the ledge of a baker's window. Oddly enough, too, whether from over fatigue or carelessness, the old gentleman had the misfortune to break one of the baker's windows. I could see him from a distance, nervously rummaging his pockets, and it seemed vainly; for when I had come up, the tradesman was insisting that the card which the old gentleman offered with a courtly air, was a poor equivalent for his broken glass."

"And you paid it," said I, knowing the Abbé's generous way.

"*Une bagatelle;* a matter of a franc or two; but it touched the old gentleman, and he gave me his address, at the same time asking mine."

"Bravo!" said I, and filled the Abbé's glass.

"I remarked that we were comparatively near neighbors, and offered him my assistance. I should observe that I was wearing my *soutane* upon that day: and this, I think, as much as my loan of the franc, made him accept the offer. He was going, he said, to the Hôpital St. Louis, to visit a sick friend: I told him I was going the same way; and we walked together to the gates. The poor gentleman seemed unwilling or unable to talk very freely; and pulling a slip of paper from his pocket to show the concierge, he passed in. I attended him as far as the middle hall in the court, when he kindly thanked me again, and turned into one of the male wards.

"I took occasion presently to look in, and saw my companion half way down the ward, at the bedside of a feeble-looking patient of perhaps seven or eight and twenty. There seemed a degree of familiarity between them which showed long acquaintance, and I thought, common interest.

"I noticed, too, that the attendants treated the old gentleman with marked respect; this was owing, however, I suspect, to the stranger's manner,—for not one of them could tell me anything of him. I left him in the hospital, more puzzled than ever as to who could be the mysterious occupants of your little chamber.

"The next day two francs in an envelope, with the card of M. Verier were left at the conciergerie. As for the daughter—if he had one—I began to count her a myth——"

"You saw her at last, then," said I.

"*Attendez!* One evening at dusk, I caught a glimpse of the old gentleman entering his court with a slight figure of a woman clinging to his arm."

. —"And the foot?"

"Ah, *mon enfant*, it was too dark to see."

"And did you never see her again?"

"*Attendez* (the Abbé sipped his wine). For a month, I saw neither Monsieur nor Mademoiselle: I passed the court early and late: I even went as far as the St. Louis; but the sick man had left. The whole matter had nearly dropped from my mind, when one night— it was very late—the little bell at the wicket rung and my concierge came in to say, that a sick gentleman two doors below (and he gave in his card) begged a visit from the Abbé. It

was Monsieur Verier. I put on my *soutane*
and hurried over; the wife of the concierge
showed me up, I know not how many flights
of stairs; at the door, she said only, 'The poor
man will die, I think: he will see no physician;
only Monsieur l'Abbé.' Then she opened upon
a miserable chamber, scantily furnished, and
the faded yellow placard your eye had detected served as curtain."

I filled the Abbé's glass and my own.

"Monsieur Verier lay stretched on the
couch before me, breathing with some difficulty, but giving me a gesture of recognition
and of welcome. To the woman who had
followed me in, he beckoned—to leave: but
in an instant again—'stay!' He motioned to
have his watch brought him (a richly jewelled
one I observed), consulted it a moment: 'My
daughter should be here at ten,' he said, addressing the woman who still waited. 'If she
come before, keep her a moment below; *après*
—*qu'elle monte.*' And the woman went below. 'We have ten minutes to ourselves,' said
the sick man; 'you have a kind heart. There
is no one I have to care for but Marie: I think
she will marry one who will treat her kindly.
I think I have arranged that. All I can give
her is in the box yonder,' and he pointed to a

travelling case upon the table. 'It is very little. Should she not marry, I hope she may become religieuse. *Vous entendez?*'

" '*Parfaitement,* monsieur.'

" 'Only one thing more,' said he; 'have the goodness to give me the portfolio yonder.'

"He took from it a sheet half written over, folded it narrowly, placed it in an envelope which was already addressed, and begged me to seal it. I did so. He placed the letter, as well as his trembling fingers would allow, in a second envelope, and returned it to me. 'Keep this,' said he; 'if ever,—and may God forbid it—if ever you should know that my child is suffering from want, send this letter to its address, and she will have money; *Oui, mon Dieu*—money—that is all!'

"And the old gentleman said this in a fearful state of agitation; there was a step on the stair, and he seized my arm. 'Monsieur l'Abbé —to you only I say this—that letter is addressed to my poor child's mother! She has never known her. I pray God she never may. *Entendez vous?*'—he fairly hissed this in my ear.

"The door opened, and that little figure I had seen one day in the court sprang in. '*Mon père!*' and with that cry, she was on her knees beside the old gentleman's cot.   Ah, *mon ami,* how his old hands toyed with those locks, and wandered nervously over that dear head!   We who are priests meet such scenes often, but they never grow old; nothing is so young as sickness and death."

For ten minutes past, I do not think we had touched the wine; nor did we now.   We waited for the dishes to be removed.   A French attendant sees by instinct when his presence is a burden, and in a moment more he was gone.

"Eh, bien? Monsieur l'Abbé!"

"Ah, *mon ami,* the *concierge* was right when he told you it was the face of St. Agnes.

" 'Little one,—*cherie,*' said the old gentleman feebly, 'this good Abbé has been kind to me, and will be kind to you.'   I think I looked kindly at the poor girl."

"I know you did," said I.

" 'I shall be gone soon,' says the old gentleman.   And the poor girl gathered up his palsied hands into hers, as if those little fingers could keep him.   'You will want a friend,' said he; and she answered only by a sob.

" 'I have seen Remy,' said the old gentleman addressing her (who seemed startled by the name, even in the midst of her grief);—

'he has suffered like us; he has been ill too—
very ill; I think you may trust him now,
Marie; he has promised to be kind.' There
was a pause. He was taking breath. 'Will
you trust him, my child?'

" 'Dear papa, I will do what you wish.'

" 'Thank you Marie,' said he; and with that
he tried to convey one of the white hands to
his lips. But it was too much for him. He
motioned to have her bring him a packet that
lay on the table. I saw that he would say very
little more in this world. She gave it him.
There seemed to be a few old trinkets in it,
and he fingered them blindly, with his eyes
half closed. 'A light, Marie,' said he. The
poor girl looked about the wretched chamber
for another candle: a hundred would not have
lighted it now. I told her as much with only
a warning finger. Then she fell upon his
bosom, with a great burst of sobs. 'God keep
you!' said he.

"Ah, *mon enfant,* how she lifted those great
eyes again and looked at him, and looked at
me, and screamed—*'il est mort!'*—I can't forget."

The *garçon* had served the coffee.

"He was buried," resumed the Abbé, "just
within the gates of the cemetery Mont Par-

nasse, a little to the right of the carriage way as you enter. At the head of the grave there is a small marble tablet, very plain, inscribed simply '*A mon père;* 1845.' I was at the burial, but there were very few to mourn."

"And the daughter?" said I.

"My friend, you are impatient: I went to offer my services after the death; a little *chapelle ardente* was arranged in the court-entrance. I begged Mademoiselle to command me; but she pointed to a friend—he was the patient I had seen in the hospital—who had kindly relieved her of all care. I could not doubt that he was the person to whom the father had commended her, and that the poor girl's future was secure. Indeed, under all her grief I thought I perceived an exhilaration of spirits and a buoyant gratitude to the friend—who tendered a hundred little delicate attentions—which promised hopefully."

"It was Remy, I suppose."

"I do not know," said the Abbé; "nor could any one at the Hotel tell me anything of him. I gave her my address, begging her in any trouble to find me: she thanked me with a pressure of the little hand, that you, *mon enfant*, would have been glad to feel."

"And when did you see her again?"

"Not for months," said the Abbé; and he sipped at his *demi-tasse*.

"Shall I go on, *mon cher?* It is a sad story."

I nodded affirmatively, and took a nut or two from the dish before us.

"I called at the hotel where Monsieur Verier had died; no one there could tell me where Mademoiselle had gone, or where she now lived. I went to the Hospital, and made special inquiries after Monsieur Remy: no such name had been entered on the books for three years past. I sometimes threw a glance up at the little window in the court; it was bare and desolate as you see it now. Once I went to the grave of the old gentleman: it was after the tablet had been raised: a rose tree had been planted near by, and promised a full bloom. I gave up all hopes of seeing the beautiful Marie again." And the Abbé paused artfully, as if he had done.

I urged upon him a little glass of Chartreuse.

"Nothing."

—"You remember, *mon ami,* the pretty houses along the Rue de Paris, at Passy, with the linden trees in front of them, and the clean doorsteps?"

"Perfectly, *mon cher Abbé.*"

"It is not two months since I was passing by them one autumn afternoon, and saw at a window half opened, the same sad face which I had last seen in the *chapelle ardente* of the Rue de Seine. I went in, my friend: I made myself known as the attendant at her father's death: she recalled me at this mention, and shook my hand gratefully: ah—the soft, white hand!"

The Abbé finished his coffee, and moved a pace back from the table.

"There were luxuries about her—*bois de rose—bijouterie;* but she was dressed very simply—in full black still; it became her charmingly: her hair twisted back and fastened in one great coil; an embroidered kerchief tied carelessly about her neck—for the air was fresh—it had in its fastening a bit of rose geranium and a half-opened white rose bud: amid all the luxury this was the only ornament she wore.

"I told her how I had made numerous inquiries for her. She smiled her thanks; she was toying nervously with a little crystal flacon upon the table beside her.

"I told her how I had ventured to inquire too, for the friend, Monsieur Remy, of whom her father had spoken: at this, she put both hands to her face and burst into tears.

"'I begged pardon; I feared she had not found her friend?'

"'*Mon Dieu,*' said she, looking at me with a wild earnestness, '*il est—c'était mon mari!*'

"'Was it possible! He is dead too, then?'

"'Ah, no, no, Monsieur—worse: *mon Dieu, quel mariage!*' and again she buried her face in her hands.

"What could I say, *mon enfant?* The friend had betrayed her. They told me as much at Passy. I am afraid that I showed too little delicacy, but I was anxious to know if she had any apprehension of approaching want.

"She saw my drift in an instant, *mon ami* —(the Abbé's voice fell). I thought she clutched the little flacon with a dreary smile: but she lighted from it into passion;—'*Monsieur l'Abbé,*' said she rising, 'you are good!' —and from an open drawer she clutched a handful of napoleons.—'*Voyez donc ça, Monsieur l'Abbé—je suis riche!*' and with a passionate gesture, she dashed them all abroad upon the floor. Then she muttered '*Pardonnez moi!*' and sunk into her chair again—so sad—so beautiful——". The Abbé stopped abruptly.

From an open drawer she clutched a handful of napoleons

I pretended to be busy with a nut: but it tried my eyes. The Abbé recovered presently; —"She talked with a strange smile of her father: she sometimes visited his grave. I saw her fingers were seeking the rose, which when she had found she kissed passionately, then crushed it, and cast it from her—'Oh, God, what should I do now with flowers?'

"I never saw her again.

"She went to her father's grave——but not to pick roses.

"*She is there now,*" said the Abbé—and in a tone in which he might have ended a sermon, if he had been preaching.

There was a long pause after this.

At length I asked him if he knew anything of Remy.

"You may see him any day," said the Abbé, "up the Champs Elysées, driving a tilbury— a charming equipage. But there is a time coming, *mon ami*—it is coming, when he will go where God judges, and not man."

I had never seen the Abbé so solemn.

Our dinner was ended. The Abbé and myself took a carriage to cross over to Mont Parnasse. Within the gateway, and a short distance to the right of the main drive, were two tablets: one was older than the other by four months. The later one was quite new, and was inscribed simply "Marie, 1846."

Before I left Paris I went down into the old corridor again, of the Rue de Seine. The chamber with the little window had undergone a change. I saw a neat curtain hanging within and a workman's blouse. I had rather have found it empty.

I half wished I had never seen the print upon the snow of *Le Petit Soulier.*

FOURTH STORY

THE BRIDE OF THE ICE-KING

FOURTH STORY

THERE is not a prettier valley in Switzerland than that of Lauterbrunnen. Whoever has seen it upon a fair day of Summer, when the meadows were green, the streams full, and the sun shining upon the crystal glaciers which lie, from the beginning to the end of the year, at the head of the valley, can never forget it. I do not think it can be more than a half mile broad at its widest: and in many places, I am sure it is much less. On one side, the rocks, brown and jagged, and tufted with straggling shrubs, rise almost perpendicularly, and a stream of water which comes from higher slopes, far out of sight from below, leaps over the edge of the precipice. At first, it is a solid column of water; then it breaks and spreads and wavers with the wind: and finally, in a rich white veil of spray, reaches the surface of the meadow of Lauterbrunnen, a thousand feet below. They call it the Dust-fall.

The opposite side of the valley does **not** change so suddenly into mountain. There are slopes, green or yellow, as the season may **be**, with the little harvests which the mountain people raise; there are cliffs with wide niches in them, where you may see sheep or kids cropping the short herbage which grows in the shadow of the rocks : and there is a path zig-zagging up from the road below, I scarce know how. It would be very tiresome, were it not for the views it gives you at every turning. Sometimes from under a thicket of trees you look sheer down upon the bridge you have traversed in the bottom of the valley—so near that you could toss your Alpenstock into the brook. Sometimes the green of the meadow, and the sparkle of its stream are wholly shut out from sight, and you look straight across upon the Dust-fall, where it leaps from the cliff abreast of you, and catch sight of its first shiver, before it is yet broken into spray. As you mount still higher toward the plateau of the Ober-Alp, the pretty valley you have left dwindles to a mountain chasm, over whose farther edge, the shimmering Dust-fall seems only a bit of gauze swaying in the wind.

The first time I made this ascent from the valley of Lauterbrunnen, was many years

since, on a midsummer's afternoon. The
mountains were clear of clouds; their white
skirts and the jagged spurs of the glaciers
which lie between the peaks, and pour down
their clumsy billows of ice toward the head of
the valley, were glowing with warm sunlight:
warm and golden, the sunlight lay upon the
green slopes around me—golden upon the farther side of the meadow below, where the peasants were gathering in their July crop of hay,
and golden upon the gush and vapor of the
Dust-fall. A mountain girl from a near cottage, in the hope of a few pennies,
was singing a plaintive Swiss air, whose
echoes mingled pleasantly with the tinkle
of the bells the kids wore, upon the cliffs
above, and with the faint murmur of the stream
trailing below. And as I lay down to rest
under the shadow of a broad-limbed walnut
(how well I remember it!) the song, the tink-
ling bells, the murmur of the stream, the broad
full flush of mid-afternoon, the emerald
meadows from which came perfume of new-
mown hay, the Jungfrau warmed to its very
peak by the yellow sunshine, that sent a glory
of golden beams through every mountain cleft
—all these made a scene, and atmosphere, a
presence, where it seemed to me, a man might

dream a life out, without one thought of labor ·
or of duty.

But summers end; and so does sunshine.
Upon my last visit, after an interval of six
years, the scene was totally different. It was
not in summer, but autumn. The meadows
were brown. The walnut trees upon the slopes
toward the Wengern Alp, were stripped of
half their leaves, and through the bleached
company of those yet lingering, there went
sighing a harsh wind of October. The clouds
hung low, and dashed fitfully across the
heights. From hour to hour, fragments of
the great glacier upon the shoulder of the
Jungfrau; burst away, and fell thundering into
the mountain abysses. There was no sunlight upon either valley, or ice.

It hardly seemed the same spot of country
which had so caught my fancy, and so bewildered me with its beauty, years before. And
yet there was a sublimity hanging about the
frowning peaks, and the cold gray sky, of
which I had no sense upon the former visit.
In that sunny summer tide, the mountains, the
air, and even the lustrous glacier were subdued into quiet harmony with the valley, and
the valley brook below. Now the gray land-
scape wore a sober and solemn hue, that lifted

even the meadow into grand companionship with the mountain and the glaciers; and the crash of falling icebergs quickened and gave force to the impressions of awe which crept over me like a chill.

I began to understand, for the first time, that strange and savage reverence which the peasants feel for their mountains. It seemed to me that darkness would only be needed to drive away all rational estimate of the strange sounds which reverberated, and of the sombre silence which brooded among the cliffs. I entertained with a willingness that almost frighted me, the old stories of Ice-gods ruling, and thundering through the mountain chasms. I strode on to the little shelter place which lies under, and opposite the Jungfrau, with the timid step of one encroaching upon the domain of some august and splendid monarch. I did not once seek to combat the imaginative humors which lent a tone and a consistency to this feeling.

A terrific storm burst over the mountains, shortly after I had gained shelter in the little chalet of the Ober-Alp. The only company I found was the host, and a flax-haired German student. The latter abandoned his pipe as the storm increased in violence and listened with me silently, and I thought with some measure of awe to the crash of the avalanches, which were set loose by the torrents of rain.

"The Ice-king is angry to-night," said our host. I could not smile at the superstition of the man; too much of the same weird influence had crept over my own mind: there was a feeling born of the mountain presence which forbade any smiling—a feeling as if an Ice-king might be really there to avenge a slight. Presently there was a louder shock than usual, and the echoes of the roar thundered for several moments among the cliffs. The host went hurriedly to the door, which looked out toward the Jungfrau, and presently summoned us to see, what he called—the Maid of the glacier.

The bald wall of rock we could see looming darkly through the tempest, and the immense caps of snow, which lay at the top. The host directed our attention to a white speck halfway up the face of the precipice which rose slowly in a wavy line, and presently disappeared over the edge of the glacier.

"You saw her?" said the host excitedly; "you never see her, except after some terrible avalanche."

"What is it?" said I.

"We call her the Bride of the Ice-king,"

said our host; and he appealed to the German student, who, I found, had been frequently in the Alps, and was familiar with all the legends. And when we were seated again around the fire, which the host had replenished with a fagot of crackling fire-wood, the German re-lighted his pipe, and told us this story of the Bride of the Ice-king. If it should appear tame in the reading, it must be remembered that I listened to it first in a storm at midnight, upon the wild heights of the Scheideck.

Many years ago, (it was thus his story began,) there lived upon the edge of the valley of Lauterbrunnen a peasant, who had a beautiful daughter, by the name of Clothilde. Her hair was golden, and flowed in ringlets upon a neck as white as the snows of the Jungfrau. Her eye was hazel and bright, but with a pensive air, which, if the young herds-men of the valley looked on only once, they never forgot in their lives.

The mother of Clothilde, who had died when she was young, came, it was said, from some land beyond the Alps; none knew of her lineage; and the people of the valley had learned only that the peasant, whose wife she became, had found her lost upon the mountains. The peasant was an honest man, and mourned for the mother of Clothilde, because she had shared his labors, and had lighted pleasantly the solitary path of his life. But Clothilde clung with a mysterious tenderness to her memory, and believed always that she would find her again—where her father had found her—upon the mountains. It was in vain they showed her the grave where her mother lay buried, in the village church-yard.

"Ah, no,—not there," she would say; and her eyes lifted to the mountains.

Yet no one thought Clothilde crazed; not a maiden of all the village of Lauterbrunnen performed better her household cares than the beautiful Clothilde. Not one could so swiftly ply the distaff; not one could show such a store of white cloth, woven from the mountain flax. She planted flowers by the door of her father's cottage; she provided all his comforts; she joined with the rest in the village balls; but, unlike all the maidens of the village, she would accept no lover. There were those who said that her smiles were all cold smiles, and that her heart was icy. But these were disappointed ones; and had never known of the tears she shed when she thought of her mother, who was gone.

THE BRIDE OF THE ICE-KING

The father, plain peasant that he was, mourned in his heart when he thought how Clothilde was the only maiden of the village who had no lover; and he feared greatly, as the years flew swiftly over him, for the days that were to come, when Clothilde would have none to watch over her, and none to share her cottage home. But the pensive-eyed Clothilde put on gayety when she found this mood creeping over her father's thought and cheered him with the light songs she had learned from the village girls. Yet her heart was not in the light songs; and she loved more to revel in the wild legends of the mountains. Deeper things than came near to the talk of the fellow-villagers, wakened the fancy of the pensive-eyed Clothilde. Whether it came from dreamy memories of the lost mother, or daily companionship with the glaciers, which she saw from her father's door, certain it was, that her thought went farther and wider than the thoughts of those around her.

Even the lessons she learned from the humble curé of the village, were all colored by her vagrant fancy; and though she kneeled, as did the father and the good curé, before the image at the altar of the village church, she seemed to see HIM plainer in the mountains: and there was a sacredness in the pine-woods upon the slope of the hill, and in the voice of the avalanches of spring, which called to her mind, a quicker sense of the Divine presence and power, than the church chalices or the rosary.

Now the father of Clothilde had large flocks, for a village peasant. Fifty of his kids fed upon the herbage which grew on the mountain ledges; and half a score of dun cows came every night to his chalet, from the pasture-grounds which were watered by the spray of the Dust-fall. Many of the young villagers would have gladly won Clothilde to some token of love; but ever her quiet, pale face, as she knelt in the village church, awed them to silence; and ever her gentle manner, as she clung to the arm of the old herdsman, her father, made them vow new vows to conquer the village beauty. In times of danger, or in times when sickness came to the chalets of the valley, Clothilde passed hither and thither on errands of mercy; and when storms threatened those who watched the kids upon the mountain slopes, she carried them food and wine, and fresh store of blankets.

So the years passed; and the maidens said that Clothilde was losing the freshness that belonged to her young days; but these were jealous ones, and, like other maidens than Swiss maidens, knew not how to forgive her who bore away the palm of goodness and of beauty. And the father, growing always older, grew sadder at thought of the loneliness which would soon belong to his daughter Clothilde. "Who," said the old man, "will take care of the flocks, my daughter? who will look after the dun cows? who will bring the winter's store of fir-wood from the mountains?"

Now, Clothilde could answer for these things; for even the curé of the village would not see the pretty and the pious Clothilde left destitute. But it pained her heart to witness the care that lay upon her father's thought, and she was willing to bestow quiet upon his parting years. Therefore, on a day when she came back with the old herdsman from a village-wedding, she told him that she, too, if he wished, would become a bride.

"And whom will you marry, Clothilde?" said the old man.

"Whom you choose," said Clothilde; but she added, "he must be good, else how can I be good? And he must be brave, for I love the mountains."

So the father and the village curé consulted • together, while Clothilde sang as before at her household cares; and lingered, as was her wont at evening, by the chapel of Our Lady of the Snow, in view of the glaciers which rose in the front of the valley. But the father and the curé could decide upon no one who was wholly worthy to be the bridegroom of Clothilde. The people of the valley were honest, and not a young villager of them all but would have made for her a watchful husband, and cared well for the flocks which belonged to her father's fold.

In that day, as now, village fêtes were held in every time of spring, at which the young mountaineers contended in wrestling, and in the cast of heavy boulders, and in other mountain sports which tried their manliness, and which called down the plaudits of the village dames. The spring and the spring fêtes were now approaching, and it was agreed between the father and the curé, that where all were so brave and honest, the victor in the village games should receive, for reward, the hand of Clothilde.

The villagers were all eager for the day which was to decide the fortune of their valley heiress. Clothilde herself wore no cloud upon her brow; but ever, with the same serene look, she busied her hands with her old house-cares, and sang the songs which cheered her old father's heart. The youth of the village— they were mostly the weaker ones—eyed her askance, and said, " She can have no heart worth the winning, who is won only by a stout arm." And others said, "She is icy cold, and can have no heart at all."

But the good curé said, "Nay;" and many a one from sick-beds called down blessings on her. There were mothers, too, of the village— thinking perhaps, as mothers will, of the fifty kids and of the half-score dun cows which would make her dowry—who said with a wise shake of the head—"She who is so good a daughter will make also a good wife."

Among those who would gladly, long ago, have sought Clothilde in marriage, was a young villager of Lauterbrunnen, whose name was Conrad Friedland. He was hunter as well as herdsman, and he knew the haunts of the chamois upon the upper heights as well as he knew the pasturage-ground where fed the kids which belonged to the father of Clothilde. He had nut-brown hair, and dark blue eyes; and there was not a maiden in the valley, save only the pensive Clothilde, but watched admiringly the proud step of the hunter Friedland.

Many a time her father had spoken of the

daring deeds of Conrad, and had told to Clothilde, with an old man's ardor, the tale of the
wild mountain-hunts which Conrad could
reckon up—and how, once upon a time, when
a child was lost, they had lowered the young
huntsman with ropes into the deep crevasses
of the glacier; and how, in the depths of the
icy caverns, he had bound the young child to
his shoulder, and been dragged, bruised and
half-dead, to the light again. To all this Clothilde had listened with a sparkle in her eye;
yet she felt not her heart warming toward Conrad, as the heart of a maiden should warm
toward an accepted lover.

Many and many a time Conrad had gazed on
Clothilde as she kneeled in the village church.
Many and many a time he had watched her
crimson kirtle, as she disappeared among the
walnut-trees that grew by her father's door.
Many and many a time he had looked long-
ingly upon the ten dun cows which made up her
father's flock, and upon the green pasturage-
ground, where his kids counted by fifty. Brave
enough he was to climb the crags, even when
the ice was smooth on the narrow foot-way,
and a slip would hurl him to destruction; he
had no fear of the crevasses which gape frightfully on the paths that lead over the glaciers;
he did not shudder at the thunders which **the**

avalanches sent howling among the heights around him; and yet Conrad had never dared to approach, as a lover might approach, the pensive-eyed Clothilde.

With other maidens of the village he danced and sang, even as the other young herdsmen, who were his mates in the village games, danced and sang. Once or twice, indeed, he had borne a gift—a hunter's gift of tender chamois-flesh—to the old man, her father. And Clothilde, with her own low voice, had said, "My father thanks you, Conrad."

And the brave hunter, in her presence, was like a sparrow within the swoop of a falcon! If she sang, he listened—as though he dreamed that leaves were fluttering, and birds were singing over him. If she was silent, he gazed on her—as he had gazed on cool mountain-pools where the sun smote fiercely. The idle raillery of the village he could not talk to her; of love she would not listen; of things higher, with his peasant's voice and mind, he knew not how to talk. And the mother of Conrad Friedland, a lone widow, living only in the love of her son, upon the first lift of the hills, chid him for his silence, and said, "He who has no tongue to tell of love, can have no heart to win it!"

Yet Conrad, for very lack of speech, felt his

slumbrous passion grow strong. The mountain springs which are locked longest with ice, run fiercest in summer. And Conrad rejoiced in the trial that was to come, where he could speak his love in his own mountain way, and conquer the heart of Clothilde with his good right arm.

Howbeit, there was many another herdsman of the valley who prepared himself joyously for a strife, where the winner should receive the fifty kids and the ten dun cows, and the hand of the beautiful Clothilde. Many a mother, whose eye had rested lovingly on these, one and all, bade their sons "Be ready!" Clothilde alone seemed careless of those, who on the festal day, were to become her champions; and ever she passed undisturbed through her daily round of cares, kneeling in the village church, singing the songs that gladdened her father's heart, and lingering at the sunset hour, by the chapel of Our Lady of the Snow, whence she saw the glaciers and the mountain-tops glowing with the rich, red light from the west.

Upon the night before the day of the village fête, it happened that she met the brave young hunter, Conrad, returning from the hills, with a chamois upon his shoulders. He saluted her, as was his wont, and would have followed at respectful distance; but Clothilde beckoned his approach.

"Conrad," said she, "you will contend with the others at the fête to-morrow?"

"I will be there," said Conrad; "and—please the blessed Virgin—I will win such prize as was never won before."

"Conrad Friedland, I know that you are brave, and that you are strong. Will you not be generous also? Swear to me that if you are the winner in to-morrow's sports, you will not claim the reward which my father has promised to the bravest, for a year and a day."

"You ask what is hard," said Conrad. "When the chamois is near, I draw my bow; and when my arrow is on the string, how can I stay the shaft?"

"It is well for your mountain prizes, Conrad; but bethink you the heart of a virgin is to be won like a gazelle of the mountains?"

"Clothilde will deny me, then!" said Conrad reproachfully.

"Until a year and a day are passed, I must deny," said the maiden. "But when the snows of another spring are melted, and the fête has returned again, if you, Conrad Friedland, are of the same heart and will, I promise to be yours."

And Conrad touched his lips to the hand she lent him, and swore, "by Our Lady of the Snow," that, for a year and a day, he would make no claim to the hand of Clothilde, though he were twice the winner.

The morning was beautiful which ushered in the day of the fêtes. The maidens of the village were arrayed in their gayest dresses, and the young herdsmen of the valley had put on their choicest finery. The sports were held upon a soft bit of meadow-land at the foot of the great glacier which rises in the front of Lauterbrunnen. A barrier of earth and rocks, clothed with fir-trees, separated the green meadow from the crystal mountain which gleamed above. All the people of the village were assembled; and many a young hunter or herdsman from the plains of Interlaken, or from the borders of the Brienzer-See, or from the farther vale of Grindelwald. But Conrad had no fear of these; already on many a day of fête, he had measured forces with them, and had borne off the prizes, whether in wrestling or in the cast of the boulders.

This day he had given great care to his dress; a jerkin of neatly tanned chamois-leather set off his muscular figure, and it was dressed upon the throat and upon the front with those rare furs of the mountains, which betokened his huntsman's craft. Many a village maiden wished that day she held the place of Clothilde, and that she, too, might have such champion as the brown-haired Conrad. A rich cap of lace, worked by the village hands, was around the forehead of Clothilde; and to humor the pride of the old man, her father, she had added the fairest flowers which grew by the cottage door. But, fair as the flowers were, the face of Clothilde was fairer.

She sat between the old herdsman and the curé, upon one of the rustic benches which circled the plateau of green, where the sports were held. Tall poles of hemlock or of fir, dressed with garlands of Alpine laurel, stood at the end of the little arena, where the valley champions were to contend. Among these were some whose strong arms and lithe figures promised a hard struggle to the hopeful Conrad; and there were jealous ones who would have been glad to humble the pretensions of one so favored by the village maidens, as the blue-eyed hunter, Friedland. Many looks turned curiously toward the bench, where sat the village belle, whose fortunes seemed to hang upon the fate of the day; but her brow was calm; and there, as ever, she was watchful of the comfort of the old man, her father. Half of the games had passed over indeed before she showed any anxiety in the issue of the contest. Conrad, though second in some of the lesser sports, had generally kept the first rank; and the more vigorous trials to come would test his rivals more seriously, and would, he believed, give him a more decided triumph.

When the wrestlers were called, there appeared a stout herdsman from the valley of Grindelwald, who was the pride of his village, and who challenged boldly the hunter, Conrad. He was taller and seemed far stronger than the champion of Lauterbrunnen; and there were those—the old herdsman among them—who feared greatly that a stranger would carry off the prize. But the heart of the hunter was fired by the sight of Clothilde, now bending an eager look upon the sports. He accepted the challenge of the stout herdsman, and they grappled each other in the mountain way. The stranger was the stronger; but the limbs of Conrad were as supple and lithe as those of a leopard. For a long time the struggle was doubtful. The peasants of

Grindelwald cheered the brawny herdsman; and the valley rang with the answering shouts of the men of Lauterbrunnen. And they who were near, say that Clothilde grew pale, and clutched eagerly the arm of the curé—but resumed her old quietude when at last, the match ended, with the cry of "Lauterbrunnen for ever!"

After this came the cast of the boulders. One after another, the younger men made their trial, and the limit of each throw was marked by a willow wand, while in the cleft of each wand fluttered a little pennant ribbon, bestowed by well-wishing maidens.

Conrad, taking breath after his wrestling match, advanced composedly to his place at the head of the arena, where stood the fir saplings with the laurel wreaths. He lifted the largest of the boulders with ease, and, giving it a vigorous cast, retired unconcerned. The blue strip of ribbon which presently marked its fall, was far in advance of the rest. Again there was a joyous shout. The men of Grindelwald cried out loudly for their champion; but his arm was tired, and his throw was scarce even with the second of the men of Lauterbrunnen. Again the shout rose louder than before, and Conrad Friedland was de-

clared by the village umpires of the fête to be
the victor; and by will of the old herdsman,
to be the accepted lover of the beautiful Clothilde. They led him forward to the stand
where sat the curé, between the old herdsman
and the herdsman's daughter. Clothilde grew
suddenly pale. Would Conrad keep his oath?

Fear may have confused him, or fatigue
may have forbid his utterance; but he reached
forth his hand for the guerdon of the day, and
the token of betrothal.

Just then an Alpine horn sounded long and
clear, and the echoes lingered among the cliffs
and in the spray of the Dust-fall. It was the
call of a new challenger. By the laws of the
fête, the games were open until sunset, and
the new-comer could not be denied. None had
seen him before. His frame was slight, but
firmly knit; his habit was of the finest white
wool, closed at the throat with rich white furs,
and caught together with latchets of silver.
His hair and beard were of a light flaxen color,
and his chamois boots were clamped and
spiked with polished steel, as if he had crossed
the glacier. It was said by those near whom
he passed, that a cold current of air followed
him, and that his breath was frosted on his
beard, even under the mild sun of May. He

said no word to any; but advancing with a stately air to the little plateau where the fir spars stood crowned with their laurel garlands, he seized upon a fragment of rock larger than any had yet thrown, and cast it far beyond the mark where the blue pennant of Conrad still fluttered in the wind.

There was a stifled cry of amazement; and the wonder grew greater still, when the stranger, in place of putting a willow wand to mark his throw, seized upon one of the fir saplings, and hurled it through the air with such precision and force, that it fixed itself in the sod within a foot of the half-embedded boulder, and rested quivering with its laurel wreath waving from the top. The victor waited for no conductor; but marching straight to the benches where sat the bewildered maiden, and her wonder-stricken father, bespoke them thus: "Fair lady, the prize is won; but if within a year and a day, Conrad Friedland can do better than this, I will yield him the palm: until then I go to my home in the mountains."

The villagers looked on amazed; Clothilde alone was calm, but silent. None had before seen the stranger; none had noticed his approach, and his departure was as secret as his coming. The curé muttered his prayers; the village maidens recalled by timid whispers his fine figure, and the rich firs that he wore. And Conrad, recovering from his stupor, said never a word; but musingly, he paced back and forth the length of the throw which the white-clad stranger had made. The old man swore it was some spirit, and bade Clothilde accept Conrad at once as a protector against the temptations of the Evil one. But the maiden, more than ever wedded to her visionary life by this sudden apparition, dwelt upon the words of the stranger, and repeating them, said to her father, "Let Conrad wait a twelve-month, and if he passes the throw of the unknown, I will be his bride."

The sun sank beyond the heights of the Ober-Alp, and the villagers whispering low, scattered to their homes. Clothilde fancied the stranger some spiritual guardian; most of all, when she recalled the vow which Conrad had made and broken. She remarked, moreover, as they went toward their chalet, that an eagle of the Alps, long after its wonted time of day, hovered over their path; and only when the cottage-door was closed, soared away to the cliffs which lift above the glaciers of the Jungfrau.

THE BRIDE OF THE ICE-KING

The old herdsman began now to regard his daughter with a strange kind of awe. He consulted long and anxiously with the good curé. Could it be that the mind so near to his heart was leagued with the spirit-world? He recalled the time when he had met first her mother wandering upon the mountains;—whence had she come? And was the stranger of the festal day of some far kindred, who now sought his own? It was remembered how the mother had loved the daughter, with a love that was jealous of the father's care; and how she had borne her in her arms often to the very edge of the glacier, and had lulled Clothilde to sleep by the murmur of the water which makes mysterious music in the heart of the ice-mountains. It was remembered how Clothilde had mourned her mother, seated at the opening of the blue glacier caverns, and how, of all roses, she loved best the Alpine rose. From this she made votive garlands to hang upon the altar of "Our Lady of the Snow." Did the mother belong to the genius of the mountains, and was the daughter pledged to the Ice-king again?

The poor old herdsman bowed his head in prayer; the good curé whispered words of comfort; Clothilde sang as she had sung in the days gone; but the old man trembled now at her low tones which thrilled on his ear like the syren sounds, which they say in the Alps, go always before the roar of some great avalanche. Yet the father's heart twined more and more around the strange spirit-being of Clothilde. More and more, it seemed to him that the mother's image was before him in the fair child, and the mother's soul looking at him from out the pensive eyes of Clothilde. He said no word now of the marriage, but waited with resignation for the twelvemonth to pass. And he looked with pity upon the strong-hearted Conrad, who fiercer and more daring than before—as if a secret despair had given courage—scaled the steepest cliffs, and brought back stores of chamois flesh, of which he laid always a portion at the door of the father of Clothilde.

It was said, too, that the young herdsman might be heard at night, casting boulders in the valley, and nerving his arm for the trial of the twelvemonth to come. The mother of the young herdsman spoke less often of the ten dun cows which fed upon the pasture grounds of her father, and counted less often the fifty kids which trooped at night into her father's folds upon the mountains. Yet ever Clothilde made her sunset walks to the chapel of "Our Lady of the Snow," and ever in her place, in the village church, she prayed as reverently as before, for HEAVEN to bless the years of the life of the old man, her father. If she lived in a spirit-world, it seemed a good spirit-world; and the crystal glory of the glacier, where no foot could go, imaged to her thought the stainless purity of angels. If the curé talked with Clothilde of the heaven where her mother had gone, and where all the good will follow—Clothilde pointed to the mountains. Did he talk of worship, and the anthems which men sang in the cathedrals of cities? Clothilde said—"Hark to the avalanche!" Did he talk of a good spirit, which hovers always near the faithful? Clothilde pointed upward, where an eagle was soaring above the glacier.

As the year passed away, mysterious rumors were spread among the villagers: and there were those who said they had seen at eventide Clothilde talking with a stranger in white, who was like the challenger of the year before. And when winter had mantled the lower hills, it was said that traces of strange feet could be seen about the little chapel of "Our Lady of the Snow." Howbeit, Clothilde neglected not one of the duties which belonged to her in the household of her father; and her willing heart and hand forbade that either the kind old herdsman or the curé should speak aught ill of her, or forbid her the mountain rambles.

The old mother of Conrad grew frighted by the stories of the villagers, and prayed her son to give up all thought of the strange Clothilde, and to marry a maiden whose heart was of warmer blood, and who kept no league with the Evil one. But Conrad only the more resolutely followed the bent of his will, and schooled himself for the coming trial. If they talked to him of the stranger, he vowed with a fearful oath, that—be he who he might—he would dare him to sharper conflict than that of the year before.

So, at length, the month and the day drew near again. It was early spring-time. The wasting snows still whitened the edges of the fields which hung upon the slopes of the mountains. The meadow of the fête had lost the last traces of winter, and a fresh green sod, besprinkled with meadow flowers, glittered under the dew and the sunlight.

Clothilde again was robed with care; and when the old herdsman looked on her under the wreath she had woven from the cottage flowers, he gave over all thought of her tie to

the spirit-world, and clasped her to his heart
—"his own, his good Clothilde!"

On the day preceding the fête, there had
been heavy rain; and the herdsmen from the
heights reported that the winter's snows were
loosening, and would soon come down, after
which would be broad summer and the ripening of the crops. Scarce a villager was away
from the wrestling ground; for all had heard
of Clothilde, and of the new and strange comer
who had challenged the pride of the valley,
and had disappeared—none knew whither.
Was Conrad Friedland to lose again his
guerdon?

The games went on, with the old man,
father of Clothilde, watching timidly, and the
good curé holding his accustomed place beside
him. There were young herdsmen who appeared this year for the first time among the
wrestlers, and who the past twelvemonth had
ripened into sturdy manhood. But the firm
and the tried sinews of the hunter Conrad
placed him before all these, as he was before
all the others. Not so many, however, as on
the year before envied him his spirit-bride.
Yet none could gainsay her beauty; for this
day her face was radiant with a rich glow,
and her clear complexion, relieved by the

green garland she wore, made her seem a princess.

As the day's sports went on, a cool, damp wind blew up the valley, and clouds drifted over the summits of the mountains. Conrad had made himself the victor in every trial. To make his triumph still more brilliant, he had surpassed the throw of his unknown rival of the year before. At sight of this, the villagers raised one loud shout of greeting, which echoed from end to end of the valley. And the brave huntsman, flushed with victory, dared boldly the stranger of the white jerkin and the silver latchets to appear and maintain his claims to the queen of the valley—the beautiful Clothilde.

There was a momentary hush, broken only by the distant murmur of the Dust-fall. The thickening clouds drifted fast athwart the mountains. Clothilde grew suddenly pale, though the old herdsman her father was wild with joy. The curé watched the growing paleness of Clothilde, and saw her eye lift toward the head of the glacier.

"Bear away my father!" said she, in a quick tone of authority. In a moment the reason was apparent. A roar, as of thunder, filled the valley; a vast mass of the glacier above had given way, and its crash upon the first range of cliffs now reached the ear. The fragments of ice and rock were moving with frightful volume down towards the plateau. The villagers fled screaming; the father of Clothilde was borne away by the curé; Clothilde herself was, for the time, lost sight of. The eye of Conrad was keen, and his judgment rare. He saw the avalanche approaching, but he did not fly like others. An upper plateau and a thicket of pine-trees were in the path of the avalanche; he trusted to these to avert or to stay the ruin. As he watched, while others shouted him a warning, he caught sight of the figure of Clothilde, in the arms of a stranger flying toward the face of the mountain. He rushed wildly after.

A fearful crash succeeded; the avalanche had crossed the plateau, and swept down the fir-trees; the trunks splintered before it, like summer brambles; the detached rocks were hurled down in showers; immense masses of ice followed quickly after, roaring over the *débris* of the forest, and with a crash that shook the whole valley, reached the meadow below. Swift as lightning, whole acres of the green sod were torn up by the wreck of the forest trees and rocks, and huge, gleaming masses

of ice; and then, more slowly, with a low murmur——like a requiem, came the flow of lesser
snowy fragments, covering the great ruin with
a mantle of white.

Poor Conrad Friedland was buried beneath!

The villagers had all fled in safety; but the
green meadow of the fêtes was a meadow no
longer.   Those who were hindermost in the
flight said they saw the stranger in white bearing Clothilde, in her white robes, up the face
of the mountain.   It is certain that she was
never seen in the valley again; and the poor
old herdsman, her father, died shortly after,
leaving his stock of dun cows and his fifty kids
to the village curé, to buy masses for the rest
of his daughter's soul.

"This," said the German, "is the story of
the Bride of the Ice-king;" and he relit his
pipe.

The snow had now passed over, and the
stars were out.   Before us was the giant wall
of the Jungfrau, with a little rattle of glacier
artillery occasionally breaking the silence of
the night.   To the left was the tall peak of
the Wetterhorn, gleaming white in the star-
light; and far away to the right, we could see
the shining glaciers at the head of the Lauterbrunnen valley.

FIFTH STORY

THE CABRIOLET

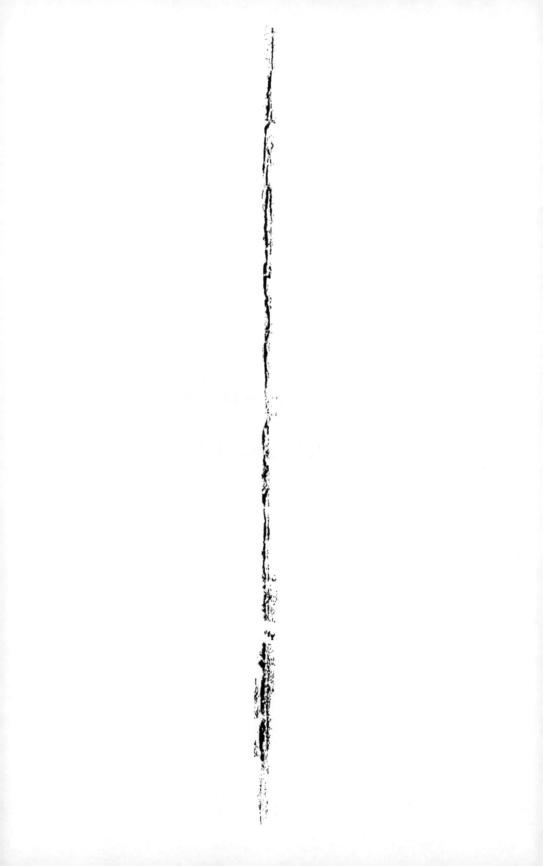

FIFTH STORY

THE CABRIOLET

A HOT July day in Paris. It is hard to be borne, and shall I persist in frying my daily dish of nettlepots under the leads of the Hôtel de Louvre, when a day will carry me where I may take breath and refreshment under the waving poplars that tuft French wayside—stiff, serried plumes that run everywhere in France out to the horizon, and keep up the illusion of army clank and marching grenadiers?

Will the reader join me in this escapade into the French country—where I will not poetize, but will tell, simply and truly, what I see, and what I hear?

Do you not love to amble, after all, with this sort of traveller, who admits you to pack with him, to eat his last meal with him, to miss the train with him, to dine with him, to see common things commonly? Are not all the great things in the guide-books, the gift-books, and the poets? Can I kindle them over?

Are they not burned to a crisp in your thought already—only ashes left,—which you spread upon your own fancies (as wood-ashes to home patches of clover) to make them grow?

Well—we (the reader and I) pack our portmanteau; 't is a small one; when you are old in travel you will always carry a small one; the more experience, the less the luggage; if you need coat or linen, you shall find coat and linen in every capital of Europe; they wear such things in all civilized countries; they sell them, too. We therefore bundle together only such things as we positively need, and giving them into the hands of a *facteur*, we direct him to carry our luggage to the office of the Diligences, a little way out of the Rue St. Honoré. We book our portmanteau there for the eastern town of Dôle, lying in the way to Switzerland, and within sight of the best vineyard slopes of Burgundy.

Our next step shall be to go around to the passage Vero-Dodat, and buy a goat-skin knapsack; it is large enough for a change of linen, a guide-book, an extra pair of woollen socks, soap and brushes, a pocket-telescope, and perhaps a miniature Tennyson—for rainy days in the mountains.

With this—a slouch, broad-brimmed hat,

a serviceable tweed suit, and heavy walking shoes, we call a cab, drive down the Rue Rivoli and the Rue St. Antoine,—cross the Place of the Bastille, and arrive presently at the station-house of the Lyons Railway. We pay a fare of twenty-five sous (we should have paid a dollar in New York), and take a ticket for Fontainebleau.

Why should we, with our hob-nailed shoes and tweed overalls, take a first-class place? Ah, the tenderly-proud Americans! so vain of extravagance—so jealous of anything like privilege—what muttons they make for the innkeepers! We have outlived this; we take a second-class seat; we pay less by a third; we see more of the natives by half; we have plenty of air; we have cushioned seats (though they may be covered with striped bed-ticking); and the chances are even that we shall have beside us some member of the Institute of France, some eminent professional man, who dislikes at once the seclusion and the price of the first-class carriage.

Away we hurtle; the houses, the trees, the fortifications, the plains, the great outstanding barracks, the white villages, drift into the dreamy distance, where the domes of Paris gleam in the haze like sparkling dandelions on

SEVEN STORIES

a dewy meadow. When we stop at Fontainebleau, after a two hours' ride, we deliver our
ticket within the station-house; and as we
shoulder our knapsack, and march into the
town, we hear the buzz of the train as it sweeps
on toward Lyons.

We stop at the inn of the *Cadran Bleu;* a
fat landlady receives us—shows us to a little
chamber, not so large, perhaps, as your attic
rooms of the New York hotels, but only up a
single flight of stairs; the floor is of red tiles,
which have been waxed that morning only,
and shine, and would seem slippery, except for
our good hob-nailed shoes. There is a dainty
bed, with coarse, cool, clean linen, and a water-
pitcher of most Liliputian make.

"Has Monsieur breakfasted?"

Of course we have breakfasted before ten
o'clock; still we will have a bite, since the ride
and the fresh air of the country have sharp-
ened our appetite.

We will have a steak *aux pommes*, and a
half bottle of Beaune, and perhaps a bit of
cheese and a plate of cherries.

"*Très bien!*" says the landlady. And when
we have washed the dust from our eyes, and
gone below, into the long *salle-à-manger*, a
tidy French girl (who would be a grisette if

she went to Paris) is laying our cloth upon an
end of the table, and we snuff the odor of the
steak, mingled with that of the jessamines
from the garden. And as we eat with sharp-
ened taste (for the Beaune is an appetizing
wine), we rejoice in the pleasant escape we
have made; we compare that quiet lunch,
within sound of the roar of the great French
forest, and only a stone's-throw away from the
magnificent home of Francis the First, with
the lunches you may be taking in the crowd of
Saratoga or Newport, amidst the clamor of a
hundred waiters, and—frankly—we pity you.
In sheerest benevolence, we wish we might
single out a pretty face and figure from the
hubbub of your watering places, and place
them beside us here in the *Cadran Bleu*, and
turn out a drop of the petillant, generous
wine, to moisten the fair lips withal;—how
she would forget the hob-nails, and we—the
hoops;—how we would luxuriate in the cool,
scented air, and loiter away afterward in the
coppices of the palace garden!

As we said, the great things of travel are
all familiar; we leave them utterly; we pass
through the Palace-yard—away from the com-
panies of strangers who are passing in and out
of the royal apartments—and loiter on along

the terrace, to the parapet that skirts the garden pond. We sit there, idly nicking our hobnailed shoes against the wall, looking over to the rich sweep of lawn and clumps of shrubbery that stretch away from the farther shore. We buy a cake from an old woman, and break it, and fling it to the fishes; these come crowding to the bait by hundreds—heavy, lumbering carp, who have lived in those waters these fifty years, perhaps a century, and may have risen to catch bread-crumbs from the hand of some pretty Dauphiness in the days gone. There are hoary veterans among them, wagging their tails gravely, and blotched over with gray spots, who it is said, date back as far as the times of Francis the First. What a quiet, serene life they must have passed! How much more royally than kings they have braved the storms and the weaknesses of age! The air is delightfully cool; the fragrance of a thousand flowering things is on it; the shadow of the farther trees falls heavy on the water. There are worse places to loiter in than the gardens of Fontainebleau.

What, now, if we wander away into the forest, comparing, as we go, the nibbling, ancient fishes of the pool, to that bait-seeking fry we have seen in other times and other watering-

places—fat, dowdy dowagers; brisk young
misses, in shoals; bright-waistcoated bucks—
all disporting like the carp—coming by turns
to the surface—making a little break and a
few eddies—catching at floating crumbs—and
retiring, when the season is over, to hibernate
under some overhanging roof-tree which they
call Home?

Oaks, beeches, tangled undergrowth, moss
under-foot, gray boulders, long vistas of high-
way stretching to a low horizon; artists sketching on camp-stools; Mr. Smith, and wife and
daughter, driving in a crazy phaeton (wife
and daughter wearing green frights, and reading Mr. Murray)—all these we see, as we
loiter on through the paths of the forest. We
make three leagues of tramp by sundown, and
are ready for our dinner at the *Cadran Bleu;*
Mr. Smith and wife and daughter are just
finishing theirs, at the end of the long table.
They mistake our nationality, and remark
somewhat freely upon French taste in matters
of diet. They are apparently from Hudders-
field; they do not once suspect that a man with
a beard, whom they meet at the *Cadran Bleu,*
can speak or understand English. So, as we
eat our *filet sauté aux champignons,* we learn
that the oaks in Windsor Park are much finer

than those of Fontainebleau; that the French beer is watery stuff; and that the Americans are not the only self-satisfied people in the world.

Mr. Smith, wife and daughter, drop away at length, we wander under the shade of the palace walls; a dragoon passes from time to time, with sabre clattering at his heels; the clock in the great court, where Napoleon bade his army adieu before Elba, sounds ten as we turn back to the inn; and from our window we see the stars all aglow, and feel the breath of the forest.

Coffee at six with two fresh eggs. If you carry a knapsack, you must carry early habits with it. The hostess brings our little bill, smilingly; we promised to tell you of commonest details, so you shall see the price of our entertainment

Lunch	2 francs.
Wine	2 francs.
Dinner	4 francs.
Room	3 francs.
Wax-light	1 franc.
Breakfast	2 francs.
Service	1 franc.

Being a total of fifteen francs. It is not over

dear, when we reckon the pleasant Burgundy we have drunk, and remember, too, that Fontainebleau is as near (in time) to Paris, as Rockaway to New York.

How the birds sing in the woods; and how the dew shines upon the nodding clover, which shows itself here and there by the wayside! After two hours' march—better than two leagues—we sit down in the edge of the forest. We have passed a woodman with his cart, a boy driving cattle, and a soldier with his coat slung over his shoulder. We shall scarce see any others till we are out of the wood.

A half hour there, under the oaks, and we are ready for the tramp again. We are only putting ourselves in walking trim for the passes of Switzerland, and so take this level country very leisurely. The little town of Fossard lies just upon the outskirts of the forest. We welcome it gladly; for by the time it is reached it is full noon. There is a straggling, white, low cottage of stone, covered with mortar, and shaded perhaps by a pear or a plumtree; then another,—like the first; a woman in *sabots* (which are heavy beechen shoes); and at last a larger cottage, with a fern bough over the door, and a floor covered with baked tiles, glossed over with grease, wax, and filth. The bough means that we may find bread, cheese, and wine there, and if not over-fastidious, a bed. The bread we take, and a bottle of sour wine; and sit at the deal table, writing there very much of what you are reading now, in our pocket note-book.

So we push on our summer jaunt; fatigue; rest in villages; strange dishes of stewed pears; Gruyère cheese; country fairs, where at eventide, we see the maidens dancing on the green sward; high old towns with toppling towers; walks through vineyards; long levels; woody copses, over which we see extinguisher turrets of country chateaux.

But all this grows tiresome at length; and when we have reached the little shabby town of St. Florentin, on the third day, we venture to inquire about some coach (for we are away from the neighborhood of railways) which shall take us on to Dôle. But at St. Florentin there is no coach, not even so much as a *voiture à volonté*, to be found; so we buckle on our knapsack, and toil along under the poplars to a little village far off in the plain, where we are smuggled into what passes for the *coupé* of a broken-down diligence. A man and little girl, who together occupy the third seat, regale themselves with a *fricandeau* stuffed with garlic. The day is cool, the windows down, the air close, and the perfume—(when you travel on the by-ways of France, learn patience).

That night we reach a town where lived that prince of boys' story-books about animals —Buffon. A tower rises on the hills beside the town, covered with ivy—gray, and venerable, and sober-looking; and the postillion says it is Buffon's tower, and that the town is called Buffon.

We desire to get to Dôle as soon as possible; so the next morning—*voilà un cabriolet!*—to catch the diligence that passes through the old town of Semur. This French cabriolet which we take at Buffon, is very much like a Scotch horse-cart with a top upon it. It has a broad leather-cushioned seat in the back, large enough for three persons. One is already occupied by a pretty woman, of some four or five and twenty. The postillion is squatted on a bit of timber that forms the whipple-tree. We bid adieu to our accommodating landlady, take off our hat to the landlady's daughter, and so go jostling out of the old French town of Buffon, which, ten to one, we shall never see again in our lives.

What think you, pray, of a drive in a French cabriolet, with a pretty woman of five and twenty? We will tell you all—just as it happened. Our cigar chances to be unfinished. "Of course, smoking was offensive to mademoiselle?"

It proved otherwise; "Oh no! her husband was a great smoker."

"Ah, *ma foi!* can it be that madame, so young, is indeed married!"

"It is indeed true"—and there is a glance both of pleasure and of sadness in the woman's eye.

We begin to speculate upon what that gleam of pleasure and of sadness may mean; and, finally, curiosity gains on speculation. "Perhaps madame is travelling from Paris like ourselves!"

"No; but she has been at Paris. What a charming city! those delicious Boulevards and the shops, and the Champs Elysées!"

"And if madame is not coming from Paris, perhaps she is going to Paris?"

"*Non plus;*" even now we are not right. "She is coming from Chalons, she is going to Semur."

"Madame lives then, perhaps, at Semur?"

"*Pardon*, she is going for a visit."

"And her husband is left alone then?"

"*Pardon*" (and there is a manifest sigh), "he is not alone." And madame rearranges the bit of lace on each side of her bonnet, and turns half around, so as to show more fairly a very pretty brunette face, and an exceedingly roguish eye.

"We are curious to know if it is madame's first visit to Semur?"

"*Du tout!*" and she sighs.

"Madame then has friends at Semur?"

"*Ma foi! je ne saurais vous dire.*" She does not know.

This is very odd, we think. "And who can madame be going to visit?"

"Her father—if he is still living."

"But how can she doubt, if she has lived so near as Chalons?"

"*Pardon*, I have not lived at Chalons, but at Bordeaux, and Montpelier, and Pau, and along the Biscayan mountains."

"And is it long since she has seen her father?"

"Very long; ten long—long years; then they were so happy! Ah! the charming country of Semur; the fine sunny vineyards, and

all so gay, and her sister and little brother—"
(madame pulls a handkerchief of *batiste* out
of a little silken bag).

We turn slightly to have a fuller sight of
her.

We knew "it would be a glad thing to meet
them all!"

"*Jamais,* Monsieur, never, I can not; they
are gone!" and she turned her head away.

The French country-women are simple-
minded, earnest, and tell a story much better
and easier than any women in the world. We
thought—we said, indeed—"she was young
to have wandered so far; she must have been
very young to have quitted her father's house
ten years gone-by."

"Very young—very foolish, Monsieur. I
see," says she, turning, "that you want to
know how it was, and if you will be so good
as to listen, I will tell you, Monsieur."

Of course we are very happy to listen to so
charming a story-teller; and our readers as
well, perhaps.

"You know, Monsieur, the quiet of one of
our little country towns very well; Semur is
one of them. My father was a small *propriétaire;* the house he lived in is not upon the
road, or I would show it to you by-and-by.

It had a large court-yard, with an arched gateway—and there were two hearts cut upon the top stone; the initials of my grandfather and grandmother on either side; and all were pierced by a little dart. I dare say you have seen many such as you have wandered through the country; but now-a-days they do not make them.

"Well, my mother died when I was a little girl, and my father was left with three children—my sister, little Jacques, and I. Many and many a time we used to romp about the court-yard, and sometimes go into the fields at vineyard dressing, and pluck off the long tendrils; and I would tie them round the head of little Jacques; and my sister, who was a year older than I, and whose name was Lucie, would tie them around my head. It looked very pretty, to be sure, Monsieur; and I was *so* proud of little Jacques, and of myself too; I wish they would come back, Monsieur— those times! Do you know I think sometimes that, in Heaven, they will come back?

"I do not know which was prettiest—Lucie or I; she was taller and had lighter hair; and mine, you see, is dark. (Two rows of curls hung each side of her face, jet black.) I know I was never envious of her."

"There was little need."

"You think not, Monsieur; you shall see, presently.

"I have told you that my father was a small *propriétaire*; there was another in the town whose lands were greater than ours, and who boasted of having been some time connected with noble blood, and who quite looked down upon our family. But there is little of that feeling left now in the French country—and I thank God for it, Monsieur. And Jean Frère, who was a son of this proud gentleman, had none of it when we were young.

"There was no one in the village he went to see oftener than he did Lucie and me. And we talked like girls then, about who should marry Jean, and never thought of what might really happen; and our *bonne* used to say, when we spoke of Jean, that there were others as good as Jean in the land, and capital husbands in plenty. And then we would laugh, and sometimes tie the hand of Jacques to the hand of some pretty girl, and so marry them, and never mind Jacques' pettish struggles, and the pouts of the little bride; and Jean himself would laugh as loud as any at this play.

"Sometimes Jean's father would come when we were romping together, and take

Jean away; and sometimes kiss little Jacques, and say he was a young rogue, but have never a word for us.

"So matters went on till Lucie was eighteen, and Jacques a fine tall lad. Jean was not so rich as he had been, for his father's vineyard had grown poor. Still he came to see us, and all the village said there would be a marriage some day; and some said it would be Lucie, and some said it would be I.

"And now it was I began to watch Lucie when Jean came; and to count the times he danced with Lucie, and then to count the times that he danced with me. But I did not dare to joke with Lucie about Jean, and when we were together alone, we scarce ever talked of Jean."

"You were not in love with him, of course?"

"I did not say so," said madame. "But he was handsomer than any of the young men we saw; and I so young—never mind!

"You do not know how jealous I became. We had a room together, Lucie and I, and often in the night I would steal to her bed and listen, to find if she ever whispered anything in her dreams; and sometimes when I came in at evening, I would find her weeping. I remember I went to her once, and put my arm softly around her neck, and asked her what it was that troubled her; and she only sobbed. I asked her if I had offended her. 'You!' said she, *'ma sœur, ma mignonne!'* and she laid her head upon my shoulder, and cried more than ever; and I cried too.

"So matters went on, and we saw, though we did not speak to each other of it, that Jean came to see us more and more rarely, and looked sad when he parted with us, and did not play so often with little Jacques.

"At length—how it was we women never knew—it was said that poor Jean's father, the proud gentleman, had lost all his money, and that he was going away to Paris. We felt very badly; and we asked Jean, the next time he came to see us, if it was all true? He said that it was true, and that the next year they were going away, and that he should never see us again. Poor Jean!—how he squeezed my hand as he said this; but in his other hand he held Lucie's. Lucie was more sensitive than I, and when I looked at her, I could see that the tears were coming in her eyes.

" 'You will be sorry when I am gone?' said Jean.

" 'You know we shall,' said I; and I felt the tears coming too.

"A half year had gone, and the time was approaching when Jean was to leave us. He had come at intervals to pass his evenings with us; he was always a little moody, as if some trouble was preying on his mind; and was always very kind to Lucie, and kinder still, I thought, to me.

"At length, one day, his father, a stately old gentleman, came down and asked to see my father; and he staid with him half an hour, and the thing was so new that the whole village said there would be a marriage. And I wandered away alone with little Jacques, and sat down under an old tree—I shall try hard to find the place—and twisted a garland for little Jacques, and then tore it in pieces; and twisted another and tore that in pieces, and then cried, so that Jacques said he believed I was crazy. But I kissed him and said, 'No, Jacques, sister is not crazy!'

"When I went home, I found Lucie sad, and papa sober and thoughtful; but he kissed me very tenderly, and told me, as he often did, how dearly he loved me. The next day Jean did not come, nor the next, nor the next after. I could not bear it any longer, so I asked papa what Jean's father had said to him, and why Jean did not come?

"He kissed me, and said that Jean wanted to take his child away from him. And I asked him—though I remember I had hardly breath to do it—what he had told him?

" 'I told him,' said papa, 'that if Lucie would marry Jean, and Jean would marry Lucie, they might marry, and I would give them a father's blessing.'

"I burst into tears, and my father took me in his arms; perhaps he thought I was so sorry to lose my sister—I don't know. When I had strength to go to our chamber, I threw myself into Lucie's arms and cried as if my heart would break.

"She asked me what it meant? I said—'I love you, Lucie!' And she said—'I love you, Lisette!'

"But soon I found that Jean had sent no message—that he had not come—that all I told Lucie, of what my father had said, was new to her; and she cried afresh; and we dared say nothing to her of Jean. I fancied how it was; for Jean's father was a proud gentleman, and would never make a second request of such *bourgeois* as we. Soon we heard that he had gone away, and that he had taken Jean along with him. I longed to follow—to write him even; but, poor Lucie!—I was not certain but he might come back to claim her. Often and often I wandered up by his father's old country house, and I asked the steward's wife how he was looking when he went away. 'Oh,' said she, *'le pauvre jeune homme;* he was so sad to leave his home!'

"And I thought to myself bitterly,—did this make all his sadness?

"A whole year pased by, and we heard nothing of him. A regiment had come into the *arrondissement,* and a young officer came occasionally to see us. Now, Monsieur, I am ashamed to tell you what followed. Lucie had not forgotten Jean: and I—God knows!—had not forgotten him. But papa said that the officer would make a good husband for me, and he told me as much himself. I did not disbelieve him; but I did not love him as I had loved Jean, and I doubted if Jean would come back, and I knew not but he would come back to marry Lucie, though I felt sure that he loved me better than Lucie. So, Monsieur, it happened that I married the young officer, and became a soldier's wife, and in a month went away from my old home.

"But that was not the worst, Monsieur; before I went, there came a letter from Paris for me, in Jean's own writing."

Madame turned her head again. Even the postillion had suffered his horses to get into a dog-trot jog, that he now made up for by a terrible thwacking, and a pestilent shower of oaths; partly, perhaps, to deaden his feelings.

"The letter," said madame, going on, "told me how he had loved me, how his father had told him what my father had said; and how he had forbidden him in his pride, to make any second proposal; and how he had gone away to forget his griefs, but could not; and he spoke of a time, when he would come back and claim me, even though he should forget and leave his father. The whole night I cried over that letter, but never showed it to Lucie. I was glad that I was going away; but I could not love my husband.

"You do not know how bitter the parting was for me; not so much to leave my father and Lucie, and Jacques, but the old scenes where I had wandered with Jean, and where we had played together, and where he was to come back again perhaps, and think as he would of me. I could not write him a letter even. I was young then, and did not know but my duty to my husband would forbid it. But I left a little locket he had given me, and took out his hair, and put in place of it a lock of my own, and scratched upon the back with a needle—'Jean, I loved you; it is too late; I am married; *J'en pleurs!*' And I handed it to little Jacques, and made him promise to show it to no one, but to hand it to Jean, if he ever came again to Semur. Then I kissed my father, and my sister, and little Jacques again and again, and bid them all adieu—as well as I could for my tears; I have never been in Semur since, Monsieur."

"And what became of Jean?"

"You know," continued she, "that I could not love my husband, and I was glad we were going far away, where I hoped I might forget all that had happened at home; but God did not so arrange it.

"We were staying in Montpelier; you have been in Montpelier, Monsieur, and will remember the pretty houses along the Rue de Paris; in one of them we were living. Every month or two came letters from Lucie—sad, very sad, at the first—and I forgot about myself through pity of her. At length came one which told me that Jean had come back; and it went on to say how well he was looking. Poor Lucie did not know how it all went to my soul, and how many tears her letters cost me.

"Afterward came letters in gayer temper—still full of the praises of Jean; and she wondered why I was not glad to hear so much of him, and wondered that my letters were growing so gloomy. Another letter came still gayer, and a postscript that cut me to the heart; the postscript was in Jacques' scrawling hand, and said that all the village believed that Jean was to marry sister Lucie. 'We shall be so glad,' it said, 'if you will come home to the wedding!'

"Oh, Monsieur, I had thought I loved Lucie. I am afraid I did not. I wrote no answer; I could not. By-and-by came a thick letter with two little doves upon the seal. I went to my room and barred the door, and cried over it, without daring to open it. The truth was as I had feared—Jean had married Lucie. Oh, my feelings—my bitter feelings, Monsieur! Pray Heaven you may never have such!

"My husband grew indignant at my sadness, and I disliked him more and more. Again we changed our quarters to the mountains, where the troops had been ordered, and for a very long time no letter came to me from home. I had scarce a heart to write, and spent day after day in my chamber. We were five years along the Pyrenees; you remember the high mountains about Pau, and the snowy tops that you can see from the houses; but I enjoyed nothing of it at all. By-and-by came a letter with a black seal, in the straggling hand of my poor father, saying that Jean and Lucie had gone over the sea to the Isle of Mauritius, and that little Jacques had sickened of a fever and was dead. I longed to go and see my old father; but my husband could not leave, and he was suspicious of me, and would not suffer me to travel across France alone.

"So I spent years more—only one letter coming to me in all that time—whether stopped by my husband's orders or not I do not know. At length he was ordered with his regiment to Chalons sur Marne; there were old friends of his at Chalons, with whom he is stopping now. We passed through Paris and I saw all its wonders; yet I longed to get toward home. At length we set off for Chalons. It was five days before I could get my husband's leave to ride over to my old town. I am afraid he has grown to hate me now.

"You see that old Chateau in ruins," says she, pointing out a mossy remnant of castle, on a hillock to the left—"it is only two kilomètres from Semur. I have been there often with Jean and Lucie," and madame looks earnestly, and with her whole heart in her eyes, at the tottering old ruin. We ask the postillion the name, and jot it down in our note-book.

"And your father knows nothing of your return?"

"I have written from Chalons," resumed madame, "but whether he be alive to read it, I do not know."

And she begins now to detect the cottages, on which in this old country ten years would make but little difference. The roofs are covered over with that dappled moss you see in Watteau's pictures, and the high stone courtyards are gray with damp and age.

"*La voilà!*" at length exclaims madame, clapping her hands; and in the valley into which we have just turned, and are now crickcracking along in the crazy old cabriolet, appears the tall spire of Semur. A brown tower or two flank it, and there is a group of gray roofs mingled with the trees.

Madame keeps her hands clasped and is silent.

The postillion gives his hat a jaunty air, and crosses himself as we pass a church by the way; and the farmeries pass us one by one; then come the paved streets, and the pigs, and the turbaned women in *sabots,* and boys' eyes, all intent; and thick houses, and provincial shops.

"The same dear old town of Semur!" says our female companion. And with a crack and a rumble, and a jolt, we are presently at the door of the inn.

The woman runs her eyes hastily over the inn loungers; apparently she is dissatisfied. We clamber down and assist her to dismount.

"Shall we make any inquiries for her?"

"Oh, Mon Dieu! j'ai trop de peur!" She is afraid to ask; she will go see; and away she starts—turns—throws back her veil—asks pardon—"we have been so kind"—bids God bless us—waves her hand and disappears around an angle of the old inn.

'T is the last we see of her; for, in ten minutes we are rattling away toward Dôle and the Juras.

SIXTH STORY

THE COUNT PESARO

SIXTH STORY

THE COUNT PESARO

I AM living in a garden, in the middle of the water. Old arbors, made from trellised poles, which are blackened with storms and with years, stretch down through the centre of this garden, and are covered over with the interlacing limbs of Lombard grape-vines. At the end of this arbor-walk—not, it is true, very long, but neatly gravelled and cleanly kept—is a low pavilion, with an embowed window which looks out upon the Grand Canal of Venice.

A painting of some Venetian artist, who lived before the garden was planted, hangs upon the wall of the pavilion, and receives a light,—on one side subdued by the jutting fragments of a ruined palace, and on the other reflected brightly from the green surface of the water.

The pavilion is built in the angle of those palace walls which inclose the garden, and which were never raised to their full height.

They offer, in their broken and half-ruined state, a mournful commentary upon the life of that dissolute republic which ended suddenly a half century ago; since which time no stone has been added to the palace walls. An iron paling, of flash appearance, swings where the palace doors should have hung. The windows are filled with mortar and brick, save the one where my pavilion looks upon the water. The huge lion heads that stand out here and there along the foundation stones, are grimy with the sea-weed which the salt tide feeds: and what should have been the court of the palace is given up to the culture of a few sour grapes of Lombardy, and to the morning strolls of a stranger from a republic beyond the ocean.

From the pavilion window, I can count the old homes of five Doges and of twenty noble Venetian families; but there is no family of either Doge or noble in any of them now. Two of the grandest are turned into lodging-houses for strangers; the upper balcony—a richly-wrought marble balcony—of the palace of the most noble Ducal family of the Justiniani, is now decorated with the black and white sign-board of my late host, Monsieur Marseille, keeper of the *Hôtel de l'Europe*. Another grand pile, which rises just opposite to me, is filled with the degenerate officials of the mouldering municipality of Venice. I see them day by day sauntering idly at the windows, or strutting with vain importance in the corridors which a century ago echoed the steps of very noble and very corrupt women. Still others bear over the rich sculptured cornices of their doors, among the marble masks and flowers, the painted double-headed eagle of the Emperor Francis; and the men I see moving with a stealthy pace over the marble stairs, are miserable Italian hirelings, who wear the livery, reverence the power, and chant the praises of their Austrian master.

All day long the gondolas glide back and forth over the green water of the canal—so near, that I can distinguish faces under the sombre canopies of the boats, and admire the neatly-gloved hands of ladies, or the martial air of our military rulers. At night, too, when I choose to linger with the blinds unclosed, I can see the lights trailing from far down by the Square of St. Mark, when no sound of the oars is heard; and can watch their growing glimmer, and presently hear the distant ripple, and see the lanterns shining brighter and brighter, and hear the oar dip nearer and nearer, until with a dash—a blaze, and a shadow of black—they pass.

The bay window of my pavilion, jutting

from the palace ruin, has marble steps leading down to the water. At ten o'clock of the morning, if the sun is bright, my gondolier, Giuseppe, is moored at one of the lions' heads, in his black boat. A half hour's easy sail along the path of the Grand Canal, will set me down at the foot of the Rialto. A score of palaces fling their shadows across the way I pass over, between the Rialto and the garden court; and a score more, catch the sun upon their fronts, and reflect it dazzlingly. But, apart from the life which the sun and the water lend to them, they have all a dead look. The foundations are swayed and cracked. Gloomy-looking shutters of rough boards close up the window-openings of sculptured marble. Newly-washed linen is hung out to dry upon the palace balconies.

Even the scattered noble families which retain the larger piles of building are too poor and powerless to arrest the growing decay, or to keep up any show of state. A black cockade upon the hat of their gondolier, with a faded crimson waistcoat for livery, and a box at the Fenice Theatre, make up the only ostensible signs of a vain rank and of an expiring fortune.

If the whim or the business of the morning lead me in an opposite direction, a few strokes of the oar will carry my gondola under the shadow of those two granite columns which belong to every picture of Venice, and which are crowned with the winged lion of St. Mark, and the patron Saint Theodore. Here is the gathering-place of all strangers and loiterers; and one may wander at will under the arcades of the Ducal Palace, or over the billowy floor of the cathedral church. But there is a tramping of feet in this neighborhood, and an active commerce in flowers and oranges, and a business-like effrontery in lame old men, who serve as *valets-de-place*, that fatigue me—that seem altogether out of keeping with the proper gloom and mould and sloth of the dying city.

My more frequent excursions are in another quarter. Traversing the garden arbor of which I have spoken, and passing through the corridor of the house which skirts the garden, I find myself upon the edge of a narrow canal, shaded by crumbling houses, which are inhabited by a ghost-like people, whom you see gliding in and out only in the gray of the morning or at twilight. The narrow canal has a foot-way by its side, along which passes an occasional bawling fish-merchant, who carries his stock in a small willow crate upon his head; cold-looking, lean women, with shawls drawn over them like cowls, and stooping and slip-shod, sometimes shuffle along the path, with cabbages under their arms, and disappear down one of the dark courts which open on the canal.

I think there must be a school in the neighborhood; for not unfrequently a bevy of boys (a very rare sight in Venice) passes under my window, under the eye of a broad-hatted priest in a long black coat. But the boys, I have observed, are sallow-faced, and have a withered, mature look, as if they had grown old before their time. They seem to have inherited a part of the decay which belongs to the desolate city; their laugh, as it comes to my ear, is very hollow and vague, with none of the rollicking glee in it which is bred of green fields and sunshine.

A funeral, on the contrary—when it passes, as it sometimes has done, after twilight, with priests in white capes, and candles flaunting a yellow, sickly light upon the still water of the canal—seems to agree with the place and with the people. The sight does not shock, as it does in cities which are alive with action or with sunshine; but, like a burst of laughter at a feast, the monotonous funeral chant chimes with the mournful habit of the place, and death seems to be only a louder echo of the life.

A little distance away, there is a bridge which crosses this canal; a dingy alley—I find, at its end—conducts through slumberous houses to a narrow quay and a broad sheet of water. Beyond the water lies the island of Giudecca; between which and the quay I am upon, lie moored the greater part of those sea-going craft which supply now all the needs of the port of Venice.

Here are quaint vessels from Chioggia, at the other end of the Lagoon, which have not changed their fashion in a hundred years. They have the same high peak and stern which they had in the days of the Doges; and a painted Virgin at the bow is a constant prayer against peril. Here are clumsy feluccas from Crete and the Ionian islands, with Greek sailors half-clad, who have the same nut-brown faces and lithe limbs you see in old pictures.

The canal of the Giudecca stretches to the westward, dividing the island of the same name from the body of the city, and then loses itself in the wide, lazy sweep of the Lagoon; there, you see little isles with tall bell-towers, and scattered lateen-rigged vessels, and square-armed colliers from England, and low-lying

233

fields of rushes—all alike seeming to float upon the surface of the water.

When the sun is near its setting, you cannot imagine the witching beauty of this scene: the blue mountains of Treviso rise from the distant edge of the Lagoon in sharp, pyramidal forms; they grow less and less in size as they sweep to the south, till finally—where the smooth water makes the horizon-line—you can see, five miles away, the trees of the last shore, seeming to rise from the sea, and standing with all their lines firmly and darkly drawn against a bright orange sky.

From this quay—a favorite walk of mine —as from a vessel on the ocean, I see the sun dying each night in the water. Add only to what I have said of the view a warm, purple glow to the whole western half of the heavens —the long shadow of a ship in the middle distance, and the sound of a hundred sweet-toned vesper bells ringing from out all the towers of Venice, and floating, and mellowing, and dying along the placid surface of the sea —and you will have some notion of a quiet Venetian evening.

Upon the bridges which spring with a light marble arch across the side canals are grouped the figures of loitering gondoliers. Their shaggy brown coats, with pointed hoods, their tasselled caps, their crimson neckties, and their attitudes of a lazy grace, as they lean against the light stone balustrades, are all in happy keeping with the scene. A marching company of priests, two by two, with their broad hats nearly touching, sometimes passes me; and their waving black cloaks stir the air, like the wings of ill-omened birds. A lean beggar who has been sunning himself throughout the day in the lee of a palace wall, steals out cautiously, as he sees me approach, and doffs his cap, and thrusts forward his hand, with a cringing side-cast of the head, making an inimitable panto-mime of entreaty; and a coin so small that I am ashamed to name it, brings a melodious "*benedetto*" on my head.

I have come, indeed, to know every face which makes its appearance along the quay of the Giudecca. A beetle-browed man, with ragged children and a slatternly wife, has lost all my sympathy by his perverse constancy in begging and in asking blessings. A dog in an upper balcony, which barked at me obstrep-erously on the first week of my appearance, subdued his bark to a low growl after a fort-night, and now he makes only an inquiring thrust of his nose through the balcony bars;

and, having scented an old acquaintance, re-
tires with quiet gravity.

Most of all, I have remarked an old gentleman whom I scarce ever fail to meet at about
the vesper hour, in a long brown overcoat, of an
antique fashion, and wearing a hat which must
have been the mode at least forty years ago.
His constant companion is a young woman,
with a very sweet, pale face, who clings timidly to his arm; and who, like her protector,
is clad always in a sober-colored dress of an
old date. Her features are very delicate, and
her hair, like that of all the Venetian women,
singularly beautiful. There is no look of like-
ness between them, or I should have taken
them for father and daughter. They seem to
talk but little together; and I have sometimes
thought that the poor girl might be the victim
of one of those savage marriages of Europe,
by which beauty and youth are frequently tied
—for some reasons of family or property—to
decrepitude and age.

Yet the old gentleman has a very firm step
and a proud look of the eye, which he keeps
fixed steadfastly before him, scarce deigning
to notice any passer-by. The girl, too—or
perhaps I should rather say the woman—seems
struggling to maintain the same indifference

with the old gentleman; and all her side-looks are very furtive and subdued.

They walk rapidly, and always disappear down a narrow court which is by the farther bridge of the quay, and which leads into a mouldering quarter of the city. They speak to no one; they do not even salute, so far as I have seen, a single one of the parish priests who glide back and forth upon the walk by the Giudecca. Once only, a gondolier, with a flimsy black cockade, who was loitering at the door of a wine-shop, lifted his hat as they passed in a very respectful manner; but neither man or woman seemed to acknowledge the salutation.

The steadfast look of the old gentleman, and the clinging hold of the young woman upon his arm, have once or twice induced me to believe him blind. But his assured step upon the uneven surface of the stones, and the readiness with which he meets the stairs of the successive bridges, have satisfied me that it cannot be.

I am quite sure there is some mystery about the couple—some old family story, perhaps, of wrong or of crime, which, in its small way, might throw a light upon the tyranny or the license which contributed to the wreck of the

Venetian State. I have hinted as much to my professor of languages—who is a wiry little man, with ferret eyes—and who has promised to clear up whatever mystery may lie in the matter.

I shall hardly see him, however, again—being now Christmas time—for a week to come.

The Christmas season drags heavily at Venice. The people may possibly be good Christians, but they are certainly not cheerful ones. The air, indeed, has a Christmas-like cold in its breath; but there is no cheer of blazing fires to quicken one's thankfulness, and to crackle a Christmas prayer for the bounties of the year.

The pinched old women steal through the dim and narrow pass-ways, with little earthen pots of live coals—the only fire which ever blesses their dismal homes. No frost lies along the fields with a silvery white coat, stiffening the grass tips, and making eyes sparkle and cheeks tingle; but the Venetian winter overtakes you adrift—cutting you through with cold winds, that howl among the ancient houses—dampening every blast with the always present water, and bringing cold tokens from the land-winter, in huge ice-cakes, which float wide and drearily down the Lagoon.

I am quite sure there is some mystery about the couple

THE COUNT PESARO

There are no Christmas songs, and no
Christmas trees. Only the churches light up
their chilly vaults with a sickly blaze of
candles; and the devout poor ones, finding
comfort in the air softened by the burning of
incense, kneel down for hours together. The
dust rests thickly on the tombs of nobles and
of Doges, who lie in the churches; dark pictures of Tintoretto stare at you from behind
the altars; the monotone of a chant rises in a
distant corner; beggars, with filthy blankets
drawn over their heads, thrust their meagre
hands at you; and a chill dampness cleaves to
you until you go out into the sunlight again.

One bright streak of this sunshine lies all
day long upon the *Riva*,[1] which stretches from
the ducal palace to the arsenal. Here is always gathered a motley throng of soldiers, of
jugglers, of Punch-players, and of the pictur-
esque Turkish and Cretan sailors. Jostling
through this crowd, and passing the southern
arcade of the Palace, you meet at mid-afternoon of the Christmas season with troops of
ladies, who lounge up and down over the
square of St. Mark's in a kind of solemn saun-
ter, that I am sure can be seen nowhere else.
Gone-by fashions of Paris flame upon the

[1] A Venetian term for quay.

heads of pale-cheeked women, and weazen-faced old men struggle through the mass, with anxious and doubting daughters clinging closely to their arms.

The officers of the occupying army stride haughtily upon the Place, eyeing with insolence whatever of beauty is to be seen, and showing by every look and gesture that they are the masters, and the others the menials.

I was looking on this strange grouping of people not long ago, upon a festal day of the Christmas season, when my eye fell upon the old gentleman whom I had been accustomed to see upon the quiet *Riva* of the Zattere across the Grand Canal. His pretty, meek-faced companion was beside him. They paced up and down with the same calm, dispassionate faces, there in the eye of St. Mark's and of the crowd, which they had worn in the view of the Lagoon and of the silent, solemn sunsets.

It is true they had now gala dresses; but so old, so quaint, that they seemed to belong, as they really did, to an age gone by. The old gentleman wore a bell-shaped hat, such as one sees in the pictures of the close of the last century, and its material was not of the shiny, silky substance of the present day, but of rich beaver. The lady, too, showed a face delicate as before, but set off with a coiffure so long gone by that its very age relieved it from oddity, and made me think I was looking at some sweet picture of a half century ago. The richest of that old Venetian lace, which provokes always the covetousness of travelling ladies, belonged to her costume, and agreed charmingly with her quiet manner, and with the forlorn air which added such a pleasing mystery to the couple.

I could not observe that they seemed nearer to friends or to kin in the middle of the crowd, than upon the silent quay of the Zattere, where I had so often seen them before. They appeared to be taking their gala walk in memory of old days, utterly neglectful of all around them, and living, as it were, an interior life— sustained only by association,—which clung to the gaunt shadow of the Campanile, and to the brilliant front of San Marco, with a loving and a pious fondness.

It is not to be wondered at, indeed, that those of old Venetian blood should cherish vain and proud regrets. They are living in the shadows of a great past. An inferior race of creatures occupy the places of the rich and the powerful. The very griffins mock at them from the sculptured walls, and everywhere what is new is dwarfed by contrast with the old.

I followed the old gentleman after a while into the church of St. Mark. He walked reverently through the vestibule, and put on a religious air that startled me. Passing in at the central door, and slipping softly over the wavy floor of mosaics, he knelt, with his companion, at that little altar of the Virgin upon the left, where the lights are always burning. They both bowed low, and showed a fervor of devotion which is but rarely seen in either Protestant or Popish churches.

I felt sure that a great grief of some kind rested on them, and I hoped with all my heart that the Virgin might heal it. Presently they raised their heads together, as if their prayers had been in concert; they crossed themselves; the old gentleman cast a look of mournful admiration over the golden ceiling, and into the obscure depths of the vaulted temple,— beckoned to his companion, and turned to pass out.

There was something inexpressibly touching in the manner of both, as they went through the final form of devotion, at the doorway. It seemed to me that they saw in this temple hallowed by religion, the liveliest traces of the ancient Venetian grandeur; here, indeed, are the only monuments of the past Venetian splendor which are still consecrated to their old service. The Palace has passed into the keeping of strangers, and idle soldiers, talking a new language, loiter under the arcades; the basins of the Arsenal are occupied by a few disabled vessels of foreign build; but in the churches—the same God is worshipped, the same prayers are said, and the same saints rule, from among the urns of the fathers the devotions of the children.

I could not forbear following the old gentleman and his companion, at a respectful distance, through the neighboring alleys. They glided before me like some spectral inhabitants of the ancient city, who had gloried in its splendor, and who had come back to mourn over its decay. Without a thought of tracing them to their home, and indeed without any distinctness of intent, save only the chase of a phantom thought, I followed them through alley after alley. The paving stones were damp and dark; the cornices of the houses almost met overhead. The murmur of the voices upon the Square of St. Mark's died away in the distance. The echoes of a few scattered foot-falls alone broke the silence.

Sometimes I lost sight of them at an angle of the narrow street, and presently came again in full view of the old gentleman, resolutely striding on. I cannot tell how far it was from St. Mark's, when they stopped at a tall doorway in the Calle Justiniana. I had passed that way before, and had remarked an ancient bronze knocker which hung upon the door, of rich Venetian sculpture. I had even entertained the sacrilegious thought of negotiating with the porter, or whoever might be the owner, for its purchase.

A shrill voice from above responded to the summons of the old gentleman, and with a click the latch flew back and the door stood ajar. I came up in time to catch a glimpse of the little square court within. It was like that of most of the old houses of Venice. A cistern curbing, richly wrought out of a single block of Istrian marble, stood in the centre, set off with grotesque heads of cherubs and of saints. The paving stones were green and mossy, save one narrow pathway, which led over them to the cistern. The stairway, upon one side of the court, was high and steep; the balustrade was adorned with battered figures of lions' heads and of griffins; at the landing-place was an open balcony, from which lofty windows, with the rich, pointed Venetian tops, opened upon the principal suite of the house. But all of these were closed with rough board shutters, here and there slanting from their hinges, and showing broken panes of glass, and the disorder of a neglected apartment. A fragment of a faded fresco still flamed within the balcony between the windows.

Only upon the floor above was there any sign of life. There I caught a glimpse of a white curtain, a cat dozing in a half-opened window, and of a pot of flowers.

I conjectured how it was: proud birth and poverty were joined in the old man. The great halls of the house, which were once festive, were utterly deserted. The sun, which reached only to the upper rooms, brought a little warmth with it. No fire was made to drive away the damps below.

A few pictures, it may be, remained upon the walls of the closed rooms, the work of esteemed artists, showing forth some scene of battle or of state, in which the founders of the house had reaped honors from the Republic. But the richly carved tables and quaint old chairs, had, I did not doubt, slipped away one by one to some Jew furniture-vender living near, who had preyed with fawning and with profit upon the old gentleman's humbled condition.

The daughter, too—if indeed the young woman were his daughter—had, I doubted not, slipped old fragments of Venetian lace into her reticule, on days of bitter cold or of casual illness, to exchange against some little comfort for the old gentleman.

I knew, indeed, that in this way much of the rich cabinet-work, for which the Venetian artisans were so famous two hundred years ago, had gone to supply the modern palaces of Russian nobles by Moscow and Novgorod.

Old time friendships, I knew, too often went to wreck in the midst of such destitution; and there are those of ancient lineage living in Venice very lonely and deserted, only because their pride forbids that a friend should witness the extent of their poverty. Yet even these make some exterior show of dignity; they put black cockades upon the hats of their servants, or, by a little judicious management, they make their solitary fag of all work do duty in a faded livery at the stern of a gondola. They have, moreover, many of them, their little remnants of country property, in the neighborhood of Oderzo or Padua, where they go to economize the summer months, and balance a carnival season at the Fenice, by living upon vegetable diet, and wearing out the faded finery of the winter.

But the old gentleman about whom I now felt myself entertaining a deep concern, seemed to be even more friendless and pitiable than these. He appeared to commune only with the phantoms of the past; and I must say that I admired his noble indifference to the degenerate outcasts around him.

My ferret-eyed Professor made his appearance toward the close of the Christmas week, in a very hilarious humor. He is one of those happily constituted creatures who never thinks of to-morrow, if only his dinner of to-day is secure. I had contributed to his cheer by inviting him to a quiet lunch (if quiet can be predicated of a bustling Italian Osteria) in the eating-rooms of the Vapore. I had a hope of learning something from him in respect to the old gentleman of the Zattere.

I recalled my former mention of him, and ordered a pint of Covegliano, which is a fiery little wine of a very communicative and cheerful aroma.

"*Benissimo,*" said the Professor, but whether of the wine or of the subject of my inquiry I could not tell.

I related to him what I had seen in the Christmas time upon the Place, and described the parties more fully.

The Professor was on the alert.

I mentioned that I had traced them to a certain tall doorway he might remember in the Calle Justiniana.

"*Lo cognosco,*" said the Professor, twinkling his eye. "It is the *Signor Nobile Pesaro:* poor gentleman!" and he touched his temple significantly, as if the old noble had a failing in his mind.

"And the lady?" said I.

"*La sua figliuóla,*" said he, filling his glass; after which he waved his forefinger back and forth in an expressive manner, as much as to say, "poor girl, her fate is hard."

With that he filled the glass again, and told me this story of the Count Pesaro and his daughter.

PESARO was once a very great name in Venice. There was in former times a Doge Pesaro, and there were high ministers of state, and ambassadors to foreign courts belonging to the house. In the old church of the Frari, upon the further side of the Grand Canal, is a painting of Titian's, in which a family of the Pesaro appears kneeling before the blessed Virgin. A gorgeously-sculptured palace between the Rialto and the Golden House is still known as the Pesaro Palace; but the family which built it, and which dwelt there, has long since lost all claim to its cherubs and griffins; only the crumbling mansion where lives the old Count and his daughter now boasts any living holders of the Pesaro name.

These keep mostly upon the topmost floor of the house, where a little sunshine finds its way, and plays hospitably around the flower-pots which the daughter has arranged upon a ledge of the window. Below—as I had thought—the rooms are dark and dismal. The rich furniture which belonged to them once is gone—only a painting or two, by famous Venetian artists, now hang upon the walls. They are portraits of near relations, and the broken old gentleman, they say, lingers for hours about them in gloomy silence.

So long ago as the middle of the last century the family had become small, and reduced in wealth. The head of the house, however, was an important member of the State, and was suspected (for such things were never known in Venice) to have a voice in the terrible Council of Three.

This man, the Count Giovanni Pesaro, whose manner was stern, and whose affections seemed all of them to have become absorbed in the mysteries of the State, was a widower. There were stories that even the Countess in her life-time had fallen under the suspicions of the Council of Inquisition, and that the silent husband either could not or would not guard her from the cruel watch which destroyed her happiness and shortened her days.

She left two sons, Antonio and Enrico. By a rule of the Venetian State not more than one son of a noble family was allowed to marry, except their fortune was great enough to maintain the dignity of a divided household. The loss of Candia and the gaming-tables of the Ridotto had together so far diminished the wealth of the Count Pesaro, that Antonio alone was privileged to choose a bride, and under the advice of a State which exercised a more than fatherly interest in those matters he was very early betrothed to a daughter of the Contarini.

But Antonio wore a careless and dissolute habit of life; he indulged freely in the licentious intrigues of Venice, and showed little respect for the claims which bound him to a noble maiden, whom he had scarcely seen.

Enrico, the younger son, destined at ·one time for the Church, had more caution but far less generosity in his nature; and covering his dissoluteness under the mask of sanctity, he chafed himself into a bitter jealousy of the brother whose privileges so far exceeded his own. Fra Paolo, his priestly tutor and companion, was a monk of the order of Franciscans, who, like many of the Venetian priesthood in the latter days of the oligarchy, paid little heed to his vows, and used the stole and the mask to conceal the appetites of a debased nature. With his assistance Enrico took a delight in plotting the discomfiture of the secret intrigues of his brother, and in bringing to the ears of the Contarini the scandal attaching to the affianced lover of their noble daughter.

Affairs stood in this wise in the ancient house of Pesaro when (it was in the latter part of the eighteenth century) one of the last royal ambassadors of France established himself in a palace near to the church of San Zaccaria, and separated only by a narrow canal from that occupied by the Count Pesaro.

The life of foreign ambassadors, and most

of all of those accredited from France, was always jealously watched in Venice, and many a householder who was so unfortunate as to live in the neighborhood of an ambassador's residence received secret orders to quit his abode, and only found a cause in its speedy occupation by those masked spies of the Republic who passed secretly in and out of the Ducal Palace.

The Inquisition, however, had its own reasons for leaving the Pesaro family undisturbed. Perhaps it was the design of the mysterious powers of the State to embroil the house of Pesaro in criminal correspondence with the envoy of France; perhaps Fra Paolo, who had free access to the Pesaro Palace, was a spy of St. Mark's; or perhaps (men whispered it in trembling) the stern Count Pesaro himself held a place in the terrible Council of Three.

The side canals of Venice are not wide, and looking across, where the jealous Venetian blinds do not forbid the view, one can easily observe the movements of an opposite neighbor. Most of the rooms of the palace of the ambassador were carefully screened; but yet the water-door, the grand hall of entrance, and the marble stairway were fully exposed, and the quick eyes of Antonio and Enrico did not fail to notice a lithe figure, which from day to day glided over the marble steps, or threw its shadow across the marble hall.

Blanche was the only daughter of the ambassador, and besides her there remained to him no family. She had just reached that age when the romance of life is strongest; and the music stealing over the water from floating canopies, the masked figures passing like phantoms under the shadow of palaces, and all the license and silence of Venice, created for her a wild, strange charm, both mysterious and dangerous. The very secrecy of Venetian intrigues contrasted favorably in her romantic thought with the brilliant profligacy of the court of Versailles.

Nor was her face or figure such as to pass unnoticed even among the most attractive of the Venetian beauties. The brothers Pesaro, wearied of their jealous strife among the masked *intrigantes* who frequented the tables of the Ridotto, were kindled into wholly new endeavor by a sight of the blooming face of the Western stranger.

The difficulties which hedged all approach, served here (as they always serve) to quicken ingenuity and to multiply resources. The

State was jealous of all communication with the families of ambassadors; marriage with an alien, on the part of a member of a noble family, was scrupulously forbidden. Antonio was already betrothed to the daughter of a noble house which never failed of means to avenge its wrongs. Enrico, the younger, was in the eye of the State sworn to celibacy and to the service of the Church.

But the bright eyes of Blanche, and the piquancy of her girlish, open look, were stronger than the ties of a forced betrothal, or the mockery of monastic bonds.

Music from unseen musicians stole at night through the narrow canal where rose the palace of the Pesaro. Flowers from unseen hands were floated at morning upon the marble steps upon which the balconies of the Pesaro Palace looked down; and always the eager and girlish Blanche kept strict watch through the kindly Venetian blinds for the figures which stole by night over the surface of the water, and for the lights which glimmered in the patrician house that stood over against the palace of her father.

A French lady, moreover, brought with her from her own court more liberty for the revels of the Ducal Palace, and for the sight of the halls of the Ridotto, than belonged to the noble maidens of Venice. It was not strange that the Pesaro brothers followed her thither, or that the gondoliers who attended at the doors of the ambassador were accessible to the gold of the Venetian gallants.

In all his other schemes Enrico had sought merely to defeat the intrigues of Antonio, and to gratify by daring and successful gallantries the pride of an offended brother, and of an offcast of the State. But in the pursuit of Blanche there was a new and livelier impulse. His heart was stirred to a depth that had never before been reached; and to a jealousy of Antonio was now added a defiance of the State, which had shorn him of privilege, and virtually condemned him to an aimless life.

But if Enrico was the more cautious and discreet, Antonio was the more bold and daring. There never was a lady young or old, French or Venetian, who did not prefer boldness to watchfulness, and audacity to caution. And therefore it was that Enrico—kindled into a new passion which consumed all the old designs of his life—lost ground in contention with the more adventurous approaches of Antonio.

Blanche, with the quick eye of a woman,

and from the near windows of the palace of the ambassador, saw the admiration of the heirs of the Pesaro house, and looked with the greater favor upon the bolder adventures of Antonio. The watchful eyes of Enrico and of the masked Fra Paolo, in the gatherings of the Ducal hall or in the saloons of the Ridotto, were not slow to observe the new and the dangerous favor which the senior heir of the Pesaro name was winning from the stranger lady.

"It is well," said Enrico, as he sat closeted with his saintly adviser in a chamber of the Pesaro Palace, "the State will never permit an heir of a noble house to wed with the daughter of an alien; the Contarini will never admit this stain upon their honor. Let the favor which Blanche of France shows to Antonio be known to the State, and Antonio is——"

"A banished man," said the Fra Paolo, softening the danger to the assumed fears of the brother.

"And what then!" pursued Enrico doubtfully.

"And then the discreet Enrico attains to the rights and privileges of his name."

"And Blanche!"

"You know the law of the State, my son."

"A base law!"

"Not so loud," said the cautious priest; "the law has its exceptions. The ambassador is reputed rich. If his wealth could be transferred to the State of Venice all would be well."

"It is worth the trial," said Enrico; and he pressed a purse of gold into the hand of the devout Fra Paolo.

II

THE three Inquisitors of State were met in their chamber of the Ducal Palace. Its floor was of alternate squares of black and white marble, and its walls tapestried with dark hangings set off with silver fringe. They were examining, with their masks thrown aside, the accusations which a servitor had brought in from the Lion's Mouth, which opened in the wall at the head of the second stairway.

Two of the Inquisitors were dressed in black, and the third, who sat between the others—a tall, stern man—was robed in crimson. The face of the last grew troubled as his eye fell upon a strange accusation, affecting his honor, and perhaps his own safety. For even this terrible council-chamber had its own law among its members, and its own punishment for indiscretion. More than once a patrician of Venice had disappeared suddenly from the eyes of men, and a mysterious message came to the Great Council that a seat was vacant in the chamber of the Inquisition.

The accusation which now startled the member of the Council was this:

"Let the State beware; the palace of Pesaro is very near to the palace of France!
"ONE OF THE CONTARINI."

The Count Pesaro (for the inquisitor was none other) in a moment collected his thoughts. He had remarked the beautiful daughter of the ambassador; he knew of the gallantries which filled the life of his son Antonio; he recognized the jealousy of the Contarini.

But in the members of the fearful court of Venice no tie was recognized but the tie which bound them to the mysterious authority of the State. The Count Pesaro knew well that the discovery of any secret intercourse with the palace of the ambassador would be followed by the grave punishment of his son; he knew that any conspiracy with that son to shield him from the State would bring the forfeit of his life. Yet the Inquisitor said, "Let the spies be doubled."

And the spies were doubled; but the father, more watchful and wakeful than all, discovered that it was not one son only, but both, who held guilty communication with the servitors of the ambassador's palace. There was little hope that it would long escape the knowledge of the Council. But the Count anticipated their action, by sacrificing the younger to the elder; the gondolier of Enrico was seized, and brought to the chamber of torture.

The father could not stay the judgment which pronounced the exile of the son, and at night Enrico was arraigned before the three inquisitors: the masks concealed his judges; and the father penned the order by which he was conveyed, upon a galley of the State, to perpetual exile upon the island of Corfu.

The rigor of the watch was now relaxed, and Antonio, fired by the secret and almost hopeless passion which he had reason to believe was returned with equal fervor, renewed his communications in the prescribed quarter. A double danger, however, awaited him. The old and constant jealousy of France which existed in the Venetian councils had gained new force; all intercourse with her ambassador was narrowly watched.

Enrico, moreover, distracted by the failure of a forged accusation which had reacted to his own disadvantage, had found means to communicate with the scheming Fra Paolo. The suspicions of the Contarini family were secretly directed against the neglectful Antonio. His steps were dogged by the spies of a powerful and revengeful house. Accusations again found their way into the Lion's Mouth. Proofs were too plain and palpable to be rejected. The son of Pesaro had offended by disregarding engagements authorized and advised by the State. He had offended in projecting alliance with an alien; he had offended in holding secret communication with the household of a foreign ambassador.

The offence was great, and the punishment imminent. An inquisitor who alleged excuses for the crimes of a relative was exposed to the charge of complicity. He who wore the crimson robe in the Council of the Inquisition was therefore silent. The mask, no less than the severe control which every member of the secret council exerted over his milder nature, concealed the struggle going on in the bosom of the old Count Pesaro. The fellow-councillors had already seen the sacrifice of one son; they could not doubt his consent to that of the second. But the offence was now greater, and the punishment would be weightier.

Antonio was the last scion of the noble house of which the inquisitor was chief, and the father triumphed at length over the minister of State; yet none in the secret Council could perceive the triumph. None knew better than a participant in that mysterious power which ruled Venice by terror, how difficult would be any escape from its condemnation.

III

IT was two hours past midnight, and the lights had gone out along the palace-windows of Venice. The Count Pesaro had come back from the chamber of the Council; but there were ears that caught the fall of his step as he landed at his palace door and passed to his apartment. Fra Paolo had spread the accusations which endangered the life of Antonio, and, still an inmate of the palace, he brooded over his schemes.

He knew the step of the Count; his quick ear traced it to the accustomed door. Again the step seemed to him to retrace the corridor stealthily, and to turn toward the apartment of Antonio. The watchful priest rose and stole after him. The corridor was dark; but a glimmer of the moon, reflected from the canal, showed him the tall figure of the Count entering the door of his son.

Paternal tenderness had not been characteristic of the father, and the unusual visit excited the priestly curiosity. Gliding after, he placed himself by the chamber, and overheard —what few ever heard in those days in Venice —the great Inquisitor of State sink to the level of a man and of a father.

"My son," said the Count, after the first surprise of the sleeper was over, "you have offended against the State;" and he enumerated the charges which had come before the Inquisition.

"It is true," said Antonio.

"The State never forgets or forgives," said the Count.

"Never, when they have detected," said Antonio.

"They know all," said the father.

"Who know all?" asked Antonio earnestly.

"The Council of Three."

"You know it?"

The Count stooped to whisper in his ear.

Antonio started with terror: he knew of the popular rumor which attributed to his father great influence in the State, but never until then did the truth come home to him, that he was living under the very eye of one of that mysterious Council, whose orders made even the Doge tremble.

"Already," pursued the Count, "they determine your punishment: it will be severe; how severe I cannot tell; perhaps——"

"Banishment?"

"It may be worse, my son;" and the Count was again the father of his child, folding to his heart, perhaps for the last time, what was dearer to him now than the honor or the safety of the State.

But it was not for tearful sympathy only that the Count had made this midnight visit. There remained a last hope of escape. The arrest of Antonio might follow in a day, or in two. Meantime the barges of the State were subject to orders penned by either member of the Council.

It was arranged that a State barge should be sent to receive Antonio upon the following night, to convey him a captive to the Ducal Palace. As if to avoid observation, the barge should be ordered to pass by an unfrequented part of the city. The *sbirri* of the quarter should receive counter orders to permit no boat to pass the canals. In the delay and altercation Antonio should make his way to a given place of refuge, where a swift gondola (he would know it by a crimson pennant at the bow) should await him, to transport the fugitive beyond the Lagoon.

His own prudence would command horses upon the Padua shore, and escape might be secured. Further intercourse with the Count would be dangerous, and open to suspicion; and father and son bade adieu—it might be forever.

The priest slipped to his lair, in his corner of the wide Pesaro Palace; and the Count also went to such repose as belongs to those on whom rest the cares and the crimes of empire.

A day more only in Venice, for a young patrician whose gay life had made thirty years glide fast, was very short. There were many he feared to leave; and there was one he dared not leave. The passion, that grew with its pains, for the fair Blanche, had ripened into a tempest of love. The young stranger had yielded to its sway; and there lay already that bond between them which even Venetian honor scorned to undo.

In hurried words, but with the fever of his feelings spent on the letter, he wrote to Blanche. He told her of his danger, of the hopelessness of his stay, of the punishment that threatened. He claimed that sacrifice of her home which she had already made of her heart. Her oarsmen were her slaves. The Lagoon was not so wide as the distance which a day might place between them forever. He prayed her as she loved him, and by the oaths already plighted upon the Venetian waters, to meet him upon the further shore toward Padua. He asked the old token, from the window of the palace opposite, which had given him promise in days gone.

The keen eyes even of Fra Paolo did not detect the little crimson signal which hung on the following day from a window of the palace of the ambassador: but the wily priest was not inactive. He plotted the seizure and ruin of Antonio, and the return of his protector Enrico. An accusation was drawn that day from the Lion's Mouth without the chamber of the Inquisition which carried fear into the midst of the Council.

"Let the Three beware!" said the accusation; "true men are banished from Venice, and the guilty escape. Enrico Pesaro languishes in Corfu; and Antonio (if traitorous counsels avail him) escapes this night.

"Let the Council look well to the gondola with the crimson pennant, which at midnight crosses to the Padua shores!"

The inquisitors wore their masks; but there was doubt and distrust concealed under them.

"If treason be among us, it should be stayed speedily," said one.

And the rest said, "Amen!"

Suspicion fell naturally upon the councillor who wore the crimson robe; the doors were cautiously guarded; orders were given that none should pass or repass, were it the Doge himself, without a joint order of the *Three*. A State barge was despatched to keep watch upon the Lagoon; and the official of the Inquisition bore a special commission. The person of the offender was of little importance, provided it could be known through what channel he had been warned of the secret action of the Great Council. It was felt, that if their secrecy was once gone, their mysterious power would be at an end. The Count saw his danger and trembled.

The lights (save one in the chamber where Fra Paolo watched) had gone out in the Pesaro Palace. The orders of the father were faithfully observed. The refuge was gained; and in the gondola with the crimson pennant, with oarsmen who pressed swiftly toward the Padua shore, Antonio breathed freely. Venice was left behind; but the signal of the opposite palace had not been unnoted, and Blanche would meet him and cheer his exile.

Half the Lagoon was passed, and the towers of St. Mark were sinking upon the level sea, when a bright light blazed up in their wake. It came nearer and nearer. Antonio grew fearful.

He bade the men pull lustily. Still the strange boat drew nearer; and presently the fiery signal of St. Mark flamed upon the bow. It was a barge of the State. His oarsmen were palsied with terror.

A moment more and the barge was beside them; a masked figure, bearing the symbols of that dreadful power which none might resist and live, had entered the gondola. The commission he bore was such as none might refuse to obey.

The fugitive listened to the masked figure.

"To Antonio Pesaro—accused justly of secret dealings with the ambassadors of France, forgetful of his oaths and of his duty to the State, and condemned therefore to die

—be it known that the only hope of escape from a power which has an eye and ear in every corner of the Republic, rests now in revealing the name of that one, be he great or small, who has warned him of his danger and made known a secret resolve of the State."

Antonio hesitated; to refuse was death, and perhaps a torture which might compel his secret. On the other hand, the Count his father was high in power; it seemed scarcely possible that harm could come nigh to one holding place in the Great Council itself. Blanche, too, had deserted her home, and perilled life and character upon the chance of his escape. His death, or even his return, would make sure her ruin.

The masked figure presented to him a tablet, upon which he wrote, with a faltering hand, the name of his informant,—"the Count Pesaro."

But the Great Council was as cautious in those days, as it was cruel. Antonio possessed a secret which was safe nowhere in Europe. His oarsmen were bound. The barge of State was turned toward Venice. The gondola trailed after;—but Antonio was no longer within. The plash of a falling body, and a low cry of agony, were deadened by the brush of the oars, as the boat of St. Mark swept down toward the silent city.

Three days thereafter the Doge and his privy council received a verbal message that a chair in the chamber of Inquisition was vacant, and there was needed a new wearer for the crimson robe.

But not for weeks did the patricians of Venice miss the stately Count Pesaro from his haunts at the Broglio and the tables of the Ridotto. And when they knew at length, from the closed windows of his palace, and his houseless servitors, that he was gone, they shook their heads mysteriously, but said never a word.

The wretched Fra Paolo, in urging his claim for the absent Enrico, gave token that he knew of the sin and shame of the Count of Pesaro. Such knowledge no private man might keep in the Venetian State and live. The poor priest was buried where no inscription might be written, and no friend might mourn.

IV

IN those feeble days of Venice which went before the triumphant entry of Napoleon, when the Council of Three had themselves learned to tremble, and the Lion of St. Mark was humbled,—there came to Venice, from the island of Corfu, a palsied old man whose name was Enrico Pesaro, bringing with him an only son who was called Antonio.

The old man sought to gather such remnants of the ancient Pesaro estate as could be saved from the greedy hands of the government; and he purchased rich masses for the rest of the souls of the murdered father and brother.

He died when Venice died; leaving as a legacy to his son a broken estate and the bruised heart, with which he had mourned the wrong done to his kindred. The boy Antonio had only mournful memories of the old Venice, where his family—once a family of honor, and of great deeds—was cut down; and the new Venice was a conquered city.

In the train of the triumphant Army of Italy there came, after a few years, many whose families had been in times past banished and forgotten. An old love for the great city, whose banner had floated proudly in all seas, drew them to the shrine in the water, where the ashes of their fathers mouldered. Others wandered thither seeking vestiges of old inheritance; or, it might be, traces of brothers, or of friends, long parted from them.

Among these, there came, under the guardianship of a great French general, a pensive girl from Avignon on the Rhone. She seemed French in tongue, and yet she spoke well the language of Italy, and her name was that of a house which was once great in Venice. She sought both friends and inheritance.

Her story was a singular one. Her grandfather was once royal ambassador to the State of Venice. Her mother had fled at night from his house, to meet upon the shores of the Lagoon a Venetian lover, who was of noble family, but a culprit of the State. As she approached the rendezvous, upon the fatal night, she found in the distance a flaming barge of St. Mark; and presently after, heard the cry and struggles of some victim of State cast into the Lagoon.

Her gondola came up in time to save Antonio Pesaro!

The government put no vigor in its search for drowned men: and the fugitives, made man and wife, journeyed safely across Piedmont. The arm of St. Mark was very strong for vengeance, even in distant countries; and the fugitive ones counted it safe to wear another name, until years should have made safe again the title of Pesaro.

The wife had also to contend with the opposition of a father, whose abhorrence of the Venetian name would permit no reconciliation, and no royal sanction of the marriage. Thus they lived, outcasts from Venice, and outlawed in France, in the valley town of Avignon. With the death of Pesaro, the royal ambassador relented; but kindness came too late. The daughter sought him only to bequeath to his care her child.

But Blanche Pesaro, child as she was, could not love a parent who had not loved her mother; and the royal ambassador, who could steel his heart toward a suffering daughter, could spend little sympathy upon her Italian child. Therefore Blanche was glad, under the protection of a republican general of Provence, to seek what friends or kindred might yet be found in the island city, where her father had once lived, and her mother had loved. She found there a young Count (for the title had been revived) Antonio Pesaro— her own father's name; and her heart warmed toward him, as to her nearest of kin. And the young Count Antonio Pesaro, when he met this new cousin from the West, felt his heart warming toward one whose story seemed to lift a crime from off the memory of his father. There was no question of inheritance, for the two parties joined their claim, and Blanche became Countess of Pesaro.

But the pensive face which had bloomed among the olives of Avignon, drooped under the harsh winds that whistle among the leaning houses of Venice. And the Count, who had inherited sadness, found other and stronger grief in the wasting away, and the death of Blanche, his wife.

She died on a November day, in the tall, dismal house where the widowed Count now lives. And there the daughter, Blanche left him, arranges flowers on the ledge of the topmost windows, where a little of the sunshine finds its way.

The broken gentleman lingers for hours beside the portraits of the old Count, who was Inquisitor, and of Antonio, who had such wonderful escape; and they say that he has inherited the deep self-reproaches which his father nourished, and that with stern and silent mourning for the sins and the weaknesses which have stained his family name, he strides, with his vacant air, through the ways of the ancient city, expecting no friend but death.

SEVEN STORIES

SUCH was the story which my garrulous little Professor, warmed with the lively Italian wine, told to me in the *Locanda del Vapore.*

And, judging as well as I can from the air of the old gentleman, and his daughter, whom I first saw upon the Quay of the Zattere, and from what I can learn through books of the ancient government of Venice, I think the story may be true.

My lively little Professor says it is *verissimo;* which means, that it is as true as anything (in Italian) can be.

SEVENTH STORY

EMILE ROQUE

SEVENTH STORY

EMILE ROQUE

IT may be very bad taste in me but I must confess to a strong love for many of those old French painters who flourished during the last century, and at whom it is now quite the fashion to sneer. I do not allude to the Poussins, of whom the best was more Roman than Frenchman, and whose most striking pictures seem to me to wear no nationality of sentiment; there is nothing lively and mercurial in them; hardly anything that is cheerful. But what a gayety there is in the Vanloos— all of them! What a lively prettiness in the little girl-faces of Greuze! What a charming coquetry in the sheep and shepherdesses of Watteau!

To be sure the critics tell us that his country swains and nymphs are far more arch and charming than any swains ever were in nature; and that his goats even, browse, and listen and look on, more coquettishly than live goats ever did; but what do I care for that?

Are they not well drawn? Are they not sweetly colored? Do not the trees seem to murmur summer strains? Does not the gorgeousness of the very atmosphere invite the charming languor you see in his groups? Is it not like spending a day of summer stretched on the grass at St. Cloud—gazing idly on Paris and the plain—to look on one of the painted pastorals of Watteau?

Are not his pictures French from corner to corner—beguilingly French—French to the very rosette that sets off the slipper of his shepherdess? If there are no such shepherdesses in nature, pray tell me, do you not wish there were—throngs of them, lying on the hillsides all about you—just as charming and as mischievous?

Watteau's brooks show no mud: why should the feet of his fountain nymphs be made for anything but dancing? Watteau's sheep are the best-behaved sheep in the world; then why should his country swains look red in the face, or weary with their watches? Why should they do anything but sound a flageolet, or coquet with pretty shepherdesses who wear blue sashes, and rosettes in their shoes? In short, there is a marvellous *keeping* about Watteau's pictures,—whatever the critics may say of their untruth: if fictions, they are charming fictions, which, like all good fictions, woo you into a wish "it were true."

But I did not set out to write critiques upon paintings; nobody reads them through when they are written. I have a story to tell. Poor Emile!——but I must begin at the beginning.

Liking Watteau as I do, and loving to look for ten minutes together into the sweet girl-face of Greuze's "Broken Jug," I used to loiter when I was in Paris for hours together in those rooms of the Louvre where the more recent French paintings are distributed, and where the sunlight streams in warmly through the south windows, even in winter. Going there upon *passeport* days, I came to know, after a while, the faces of all the artists who busy themselves with copying those rollicking French masters of whom I have spoken. Nor could I fail to remark that the artists who chose those sunny rooms for their easels, and those sunny masters for their subjects, were far more cheerful and gay in aspect than the pinched and sour-looking people in the Long Gallery, who grubbed away at their Da Vincis, and their Sasso Ferratos.

Among those who wore the joyous faces, and who courted the sunny atmosphere which hangs about Boucher and Watteau, I had frequent occasion to remark a tall, athletic young fellow, scarce four-and-twenty, who seemed to take a special delight in drawing the pretty shepherdesses and the well-behaved goats about which I was just now speaking.

I do not think he was a great artist; I feel quite sure that he never imagined it himself; but he came to his work, and prepared his easel —rubbing his hands together the while—with a glee that made me sure he had fallen altogether into the spirit of that sunny nymph-world which Watteau has created.

I have said that I thought him no great artist; nor was he; yet there was something quite remarkable in his copies. He did not finish well; his coloring bore no approach to the noontide mellowness of the originals; his figures were frequently out of drawing; but he never failed to catch the expression of the faces, and to intensify (if I may use the term) the joviality that belonged to them. He turned the courtly levity of Watteau into a kind of mad mirth. You could have sworn to the identity of the characters; but on the canvas of the copyist they had grown riotous.

What drew my attention the more was— what seemed to me the artist's thorough and joyful participation in the riot he made. After a rapid half-dozen of touches with his brush, he would withdraw a step or two from his easel, and gaze at his work with a hearty satisfaction that was most cheering, even to a looker-on. His glance seemed to say—"There I have you, little nymphs; I have taken you out of the genteel society of Watteau, and put you on my own ground, where you may frisk as much as you please." And he would beat the measure of a light polka on his pallet.

I ought to say that this artist was a fine-looking fellow withal, and his handsome face, aglow with enthusiasm, drew away the attention of not a few lady visitors from the pretty Vanloos scattered around. I do not think he was ever disturbed by this; I do not think that he tweaked his mustache, or gave himself airs in consequence. Yet he saw it all; he saw everything and everybody; his face wore the same open, easy, companionable look which belongs to the frolicking swains of Watteau. His freedom of manner invited conversation; and on some of my frequent visits to the French gallery I was in the habit of passing a word or two with him myself.

"You seem," said I to him one day, "to admire Watteau very much?"

"*Oui, Monsieur, vous avez raison: j'aime les choses riantes, moi.*"

"We have the same liking," said I.

"*Ah, vous aussi: je vous en félicite, Monsieur. Tenez,*"—drawing me forward with the most naive manner in the world to look at a group he had just completed—"*Regardez! n'est ce pas, que ces petites dames là rient aux anges?*"

I chanced to have in that time an artist friend in Paris—De Courcy, a Provincial by birth, but one who had spent half his life in the capital, and who knew by name nearly every copyist who made his appearance at either of the great galleries. He was himself busy just then at the Luxembourg; but I took him one day with me through the Louvre, and begged him to tell me who was the artist so enraptured with Watteau.

As I had conjectured, he knew, or professed to know, all about him. He sneered at his painting—as a matter of course: his manner was very sketchy; his trees stiff; no action in his figures; but, after all, tolerably well—*passablement bien*—for an amateur.

He was a native of the South of France; his

name—Emille Roque; he was possessed of an easy fortune, and was about to marry, rumor said, the daughter of a government officer of some distinction in the Department of Finance.

Was there any reason why my pleasant friend of the sunny pictures should not be happy? Rumor gave to his promised bride a handsome *dot*. Watteau was always open to his pencil and his humor. Bad as his copies might be, he enjoyed them excessively. He had youth and health on his side; and might, for aught that appeared, extend his series of laughing nymphs and coquettish shepherdesses to the end of his life.

The thought of him, or of the cheery years which lay before him, came to my mind very often, as I went journeying shortly after, through the passes of the Alps. It comes to me now, as I sit by my crackling fireside in New England, with the wind howling through the pine-tree at the corner, and the snow lying high upon the ground.

II

I HAD left Paris in the month of May; I came back toward the end of August. The last is a dull month for the capital; Parisians have not yet returned from Baden, or the Pyrenees, or Dieppe. True, the Boulevard is always gay; but it has its seasons of exceeding gayety, and latter summer is by no means one of them. The shopmen complain of the dulness, and lounge idly at their doors; their only customers are passing strangers. Pretty suites of rooms are to be had at half the rates of autumn, or of opening spring. The bachelor can indulge without extravagance in apartments looking upon the Madeleine. The troops of children whom you saw in the spring-time under the lee of the terrace wall in the "little Provence" of the Tuileries are all gone to St. Germain, or to Trouville. You see no more the tall caps of the Norman nurses, or the tight little figures of the Breton *bonnes*.

It is the season of vacation at the schools; and if you stroll by the Sorbonne, or the College of France, the streets have a deserted air; and the garden of the Luxembourg is filled only with invalids and strolling soldiers. The artists even, have mostly stolen away from their easels in the galleries, and are studying the live fish women of Boulogne or the bare-ankled shepherdesses of Auvergne.

I soon found my way to all the old haunts of the capital. I found it easy to revive my taste for the coffee of the Rotonde, in the Palais Royal; and easy to listen and laugh at Sainville and Grassot. I went, a few days after my return, to the always charming salons of the Louvre. The sun was hot at this season upon that wing of the palace where hang the pictures of Watteau; and the galleries were nearly deserted. In the salon where I had seen so often the beaming admirer of nymphs and shepherdesses, there was now only a sharp-faced English woman, with bright erysipelas on nose and cheeks, working hard at a Diana of Vanloo.

I strolled on carelessly to the cool corner room, serving as antechamber to the principal gallery, and which every visitor will remember for its great picture of the battle of Eylau. There are several paintings about the walls of this salon, which are in constant request by the copyists; I need hardly mention that favorite picture of Gerard, *L'Amour et Psyché*. There was a group about it now; and in the neighborhood of this group I saw, to my surprise, my old artist acquaintance of the Watteau nymphs. But a sad change had come over him since I saw him last. The gay humor that shone in his face on my spring visits to the gallery was gone. The openness of look which seemed to challenge regard, if not conversation, he had lost utterly. I was not surprised that he had deserted the smiling shepherdesses of Watteau.

There was a settled and determined gloom upon his face, which I was sure no painted sunshine could enliven. He was not busy with the enamelled prettiness of Gerard; far from it. His easel was beside him, but his eye was directed toward that fearful melo-dramatic painting—*La Méduse* of Géricault. It is a horrible shipwreck story: a raft is floating upon an ocean waste; dead bodies that may have been copied from the dissecting-halls, lie on it; a few survivors, emaciated, and with rigid limbs, cluster around the frail spar that serves as mast, and that sways with the weight of a tattered sail; one athletic figure rises above this dismal group, and with emaciated arm held to its highest reach, lifts a fluttering rag; his bloodshot eye, lighted with a last hope, strains over the waste of waters which seethe beyond him.

It was a picture from which I had always turned away with a shudder. It may have truth and force; but the truth is gross, and the force brutal. Yet upon this subject I found Emile Roque engaged with a fearful intensity.

He had sketched only the principal figure of the dying group—the athlete who beckons madly, whose hope is on the waste. He had copied only a fragment of the raft—barely enough to give foothold to the figure; he had not even painted the sea, but had filled his little canvas with a cold white monotone of color, like a sleeted waste in winter.

I have already remarked the wonderful vitality which he gave to mirth in his frolicsome pastorals; the same power was apparent here; and he had intensified the despair of the wretched castaway, shaking out his last rag of hope,—to a degree that was painful to look upon.

I went near him; but he wore no longer the old tokens of ready fellowship. He plainly had no wish to recognize, or be recognized. He was intent only upon wreaking some bitter thought, or some blasted hope in the face of that shipwrecked man. The despairing look, and the bloodshot eye, which he had given to his copy of the castaway, haunted me for days. It made that kind of startling impression upon my mind which I was sure could never be forgotten. I never think, even now, of that painting in the Louvre, with the cold north light gleaming on it, but the ghastly expression of the shipwrecked man—as Emile Roque had rendered it in his copy—starts to my mind like a phantom. I see the rag fluttering from the clenched, emaciated hand; I see the pallid, pinched flesh; I see the starting eyes, bearing resemblance,—as it seemed to me afterward, and seems to me now,—to those of the distracted artist.

There was a cloud over the man; I felt sure of that; I feared what might be the end of it. My eye ran over the daily journals, seeking in the list of suicides for the name of Emile Roque. I thought it would come to that. On every new visit to the Louvre I expected to find him gone. But he was there, assiduous as ever; refining still upon the horrors of Géricault.

My acquaintance of the Luxembourg, De Courcy, who had given me all the information I possessed about the history and prospects of this artist, was out of the city; he would not return until late in the autumn. I dropped a line into the Poste Restante to meet him on his return, as I was myself very shortly on the wing for Italy. I can recall perfectly the expressions in my letter. After intrusting him with one or two unimportant commissions, I said: "By-the-by, you remember the jolly-look-

ing Emile Roque, who made such a frenzy out
of his love for Watteau and his shepherdesses,
and who was to come into possession of a
pretty wife and a pretty *dot?*

"Is the *dot* forthcoming? Before you answer, go and look at him again—in the Louvre
still; but he has deserted Watteau; he is studying and copying the horrors of *La Méduse.*
It does not look like a betrothal or a honey-
moon. If he were not an amateur, I should
charge you to buy for me that terrible figure
he is working up from the raft scene. The
intensity he is putting in it is not Géricault's—
my word for it, it is *his own.*

"When he is booked among the suicides
(where your Parisian forms of madness seem
to tend), send me the journal, and tell me what
you can of the why."

In the galleries of Florence one forgets the
French painters utterly, and rejoices in the for-
getfulness. Among the Carraccis and the
Guidos what room is there for the lover-like
Watteau? Even Greuze, on the walls of the
Pitti Palace, would be Greuze no longer. It is
a picture-life one leads in those old cities of
art, growing day by day into companionship
with the masters and the masters' subjects.

How one hob-nobs with the weird sisters of

Michael Angelo! How he pants through Sny-
der's Boar-Hunt, or lapses into a poetic sympathy with the marble flock of Niobe!

Who wants letters of introduction to the
"nice people" of Florence, when he can chat
with the Fornarina by the hour, and listen to
Raphael's Pope Julius?

Yesterday—I used to say to myself—I spent
an hour or two with old Gerard Douw and
pretty Angelica Kauffman—nice people, both
of them. To-morrow I will pass the morning
with Titian, and lunch off a plate of Carlo
Dolci's. In such company one grows into a
delightful "Middle-Age" feeling, in which the
vanities of daily journals and hotel bills are
forgotten.

In this mood of mind, when I was hesita-
ting, one day of mid-winter, whether I would
sun myself in a Claude Lorraine, or between
the Arno and the houses, the valet of the inn
where I was staying, put a letter in my hand
bearing a Paris post-mark.

"It must be from De Courcy," said I; and
my fancy straightway conjured up an image
of the dapper little man disporting among all
the gayeties and the grisettes of a Paris world;
but I had never one thought of poor Emile
Roque, until I caught sight of his name within
the letter.

After acquitting himself of the sundry commissions left in his keeping, De Courcy says:—

"You were half right and half wrong about the jolly artist of Watteau. His suicide is not in the journals, but for all that it may be. I had no chance of seeing him at his new game in the corner salon, for the bird had flown before my return. I heard, though, very much of his strange copy of the crowning horror of Géricault. Nor would you have been the only one in the market as purchaser of his extravaganza. A droll story is told of an English visitor who was startled one day by, I dare say, the same qualities which you discovered in the copy; but the Briton, with none of your scruples, addressed himself, in the best way he could, to the artist himself, requesting him to set a price upon his work.

"The old Emile Roque whom I had known —in fact, whom we had known together— would have met such a question with the gayest and most gallant refusal possible.

"But what did this bewitched admirer of Géricault do?

"He kept at his work—doggedly, gloomily.

"The Englishman stubbornly renewed his inquiry—this time placing his hand upon the canvas, to aid his solicitation by so much of pantomime.

"The painter (you remember his stalwart figure) brushed the stranger's hand aside, and with a petrifying look and great energy of expression (as if the poor Briton had been laying his hand on his very heart), said: *'C'est à moi, Monsieur—à moi—à moi!'*—beating his hand on his breast the while.

"Poor Emile! The jovial times of Watteau's nymphs are, I fear, gone forever.

"But I forget to tell you what I chiefly had in mind when I began this mention of him. Some say his love has crazed him—some say no. The truth is, he is not to marry the pretty Virginie C——, one time his affianced.

"There are objections. Rumor says they come from Monsieur C——, *sous chef* in the office of Finance, and father of Virginie; and rumor adds that the objections are insurmountable. What they are, Heaven only knows. Surely a daintier fellow never sued for favor; and as for scandal, Emile Roque was what you call, I believe, a Puritan." [I do not think it necessary to correct De Courcy's strange use of an English term.]

"The oddest thing of all I have yet to tell you. This broken hope diverted Emile from Watteau to the corner salon of the Louvre; at least I infer as much, since the two events agree in time. It is evident, furthermore, that the poor fellow takes the matter bitterly to heart; and it is perfectly certain that all the objection rests with the father of the *fiancée*.

"So far, nothing strange; but notwithstanding this opposition on the part of Monsieur C——, it is known that Emile was in constant and familiar, nay, friendly communication with him up to the time of his disappearance from the capital, which occurred about the date of my return.

"Read me this riddle if you can! Is the rendering of the horrors of Géricault to restore Emile to favor? Or shall I, as you prophesied four months ago (ample time for such consummation), still look for his enrollment among the suicides?"

With this letter in my hand (there were others in my heart), I gave up for that day the noontides of Claude, and sunned myself instead along the Arno. Beyond the houses which hang on the further bank of the river, I could see the windows of the Pitti Palace and the cypresses of the Boboli gardens, and above both, the blue sky which arched over the tower of Galileo upon the distant hills. I wished the distracted painter might have been there on the sunny side of the houses, which were full of memories of Angelo and Cellini, to forget his troubles. If an unwilling father were all, there might be no suicide. Still, the expression in his copy of the castaway haunted me.

III

WHY should I go on to speak of pictures here —except that I love them? Why should I recall the disgusting and wonderful old men and women of Denner, which hang with glass over them, within the window bays of the palace of Belvidere at Vienna? Why should my fancy go stalking through that great Rubens Museum, with its red arms, fat bosoms, pin-cushion cheeks, and golden hair?

Why does my thought whisk away to that gorgeous salon of Dresden, where hangs the greatest of all Raphael's Madonnas?

The face of the Virgin is all that makes perfection in female beauty; it is modest, it is tender, it is intelligent. The eyes are living eyes, but with no touch of earthiness, save the shade of care which earth's sorrows give even to the Holy Virgin. She wears the dignity of the mother of Christ, with nothing of severity to repulse; she wears the youthful innocence

of the spouse of David, with no touch of levity; she wears the modest bearing of one whose
child was nursed in a manger, with the presence of one "chosen from among women."
She is mounting on clouds to heaven; light as
an angel, but with no wings; her divinity sus-
tains her.   In her arms she holds lightly but
firmly the infant Jesus, who has the face of a
true child, with something else beyond humanity; his eye has a little of the look of a frighted
boy in some strange situation, where he knows
he is safe, and where yet he trembles.   His
light, silky hair is strewn by a wind (you feel
it like a balm) over a brow beaming with soul;
he looks deserving the adoration the shepherds
gave him; and there is that—in his manner,
innocent as the babe he was—in his look, Divine as the God he was, which makes one see
in the child

—" the father of the man."

Pope Sixtus is lifting his venerable face in
adoration from below; and opposite, Saint
Barbara,' beautiful and modest, has dropped
her eyes, though religious awe and love are
beaming in her looks.   Still lower, and lifting
their heads and their little wings only above

the edge of the picture, are two cherubs, who are only less in beauty than the Christ; they are twins—but they are twin angels—and Christ is God.

The radiance in their faces is, I think, the most wonderful thing I have ever seen in painting. They are listening to the celestial harmony which attends the triumph of the Virgin. These six faces make up the picture; the Jesus, a type of divinity itself; the Virgin, the purity of earth, as at the beginning,—yet humble, because of earth; the cherubs, the purity of heaven, conscious of its high estate; the two saints, earth made pure and sanctified by Christ—half doubting, yet full of hope.

I wrote thus much in my note-book, as I stood before the picture in that room of the Royal Gallery which looks down upon the market-place of Dresden; and with the painting lingering in my thought more holily than sermons of a Sunday noontime, I strolled over the market-place, crossed the long bridge which spans the Elbe, and wandered up the banks of the river as far as the Findlater Gardens. The terrace is dotted over with tables and benches, where one may sit over his coffee or ice, and enjoy a magnificent view of Dresden, the river, the bridge, and the green battle-field where

Moreau fell. It was a mild day of winter, and I sat there enjoying the prospect, sipping at a *demi-tasse*, and casting my eye from time to time over an old number of the *Débats* newspaper, which the waiter had placed upon my table.

When there is no political news of importance stirring, I was always in the habit of running over the column of *Faits Divers:* "Different Things" translates it, but does not give a good idea of the piquancy which usually belongs to that column. The suicides are all there; the extraordinary robberies are there; important discoveries are entered; and all the bits of scandal, which, of course, everybody reads and everybody says should never have been published.

In the journal under my hand there was mention of two murders,—one of them of that stereotype class growing out of a drunken brawl, which the world seems to regard indifferently, as furnishing the needed punctuation-marks in the history of civilization. The other drew my attention very closely.

The Count de Roquefort, an elderly gentleman of wealth and distinguished family, residing in a chateau a little off the high road leading from Nismes to Avignon, in the South of France, had been brutally murdered in his own house. The Count was unmarried; none of his family connection resided with him, and aside from a considerable retinue of servants, he lived quite alone—devoted, as was said, to scientific pursuits.

It appeared that two days before his assassination he was visited by a young man, a stranger in that region, who was received (the servants testified) kindly by the Count, and who passed two hours closeted with him in his library. On the day of the murder the same young man was announced; his manner was excited, and he was ushered, by the Count's order, into the library, as before.

It would seem, however, that the Count had anticipated the possibility of some trouble, since he had secured the presence of two "officers of the peace" in his room. It was evident that the visitor had come by appointment. The officers were concealed under the hangings of a bay-window at the end of the library, with orders from the Count not to act, unless they should see signs of violence.

The young man, on entering, advanced toward the table beside which the Count was seated, reading. He raised his head at the visitor's entrance, and beckoned to a chair.

The stranger approached more nearly, and without seating himself, addressed the Count in a firm tone of voice to this effect:

"I have come to ask, *Monsieur le Comte,* if you are prepared to accept the propositions I made to you two days ago?"

The Count seemed to hesitate for a moment; but only, it appeared, from hearing some noise in the servants' hall below.

The visitor appeared excited by his calmness, and added, "I remind you, for the last time, of the vow I have sworn to accomplish if you refuse my demand."

"I *do* refuse," said the Count, firmly. "It is a rash ——"

It was the last word upon his lips; for before the officers could interfere, the visitor had drawn a pistol from his breast and discharged it at the head of the Count. The ball entered the brain. The Count lingered for two hours after, but showed no signs of consciousness.

The assassin, who was promptly arrested, is a stalwart man of about thirty, and from the contents of his portmanteau, which he had left at the inn of an adjoining village, it is presumed that he followed the profession of an artist.

The cause of the murder is still a mystery;

the Count had communicated nothing to throw light upon it. He was a kind master, and was not known to have an enemy in the world.

I had read this account with that eager curiosity with which I believe all—even the most sensitive and delicate—unwittingly devour narratives of that kind; I had finished my half-cup of coffee, and was conjecturing what could possibly be the motive for such a murder, and what the relations between the Count and the strange visitor, when suddenly—like a flash—the conviction fastened itself upon me, that the murderer was none other than Emile Roque!

I did not even think in that moment of the remote similarity in the two names—Roque and De Roquefort. For anything suggestive that lay in it, the name might as well have been De Montfort or De Courcy; I am quite sure of that.

Indeed, no association of ideas, no deduction from the facts named, led me to the conclusion which I formed on the spur of the moment. Yet my conviction was as strong as my own consciousness. I knew Emile Roque was the murderer; I remembered it; for I remembered his copy of the head of the castaway in Géricault's Wreck of the Medusa!

When I had hazarded the conjecture of suicide, I had reasoned loosely from the changed appearance of the man, and from the suicidal tendency of the Paris form of madness. Now I reasoned, not from the appearance of the man at all, but from my recollection of his painting.

There is no resignation in the face of Géricault's shipwrecked man; there is only animal fear and despair, lighted with but one small ray of hope. The ties of humanity exist no longer for him; whatever was near or dear is forgotten in that supreme moment when the animal instinct of self-preservation at once brutalizes and vitalizes every faculty.

Such is Géricault's picture; but Roque had added the intensity of moral despair: he had foreshadowed the tempest of a soul tossed on a waste—not of ocean—but of doubt, hate, crime! I felt sure that he had unwittingly foretokened his own destiny.

Are there not moments in the lives of all of us—supreme moments—when we have the power lent us to wreak in language, or on canvas, or in some wild burst of music (as our habit of expression may lie), all our capabilities, and to typify, by one effort of the soul, all the issues of our life? I knew now that Emile

Roque had unwittingly done this in his head
from the Medusa. I knew that the period was
to occur in his life when his own thought and
action would illustrate to the full all the wildness and the despair to which he had already
given pictured expression. I cannot tell how
I knew this, any more than I can tell how I
knew that he was the murderer.

I wrote De Courcy that very day, referring
him to the paragraph I had read, and adding:
"This artist is Emile Roque, but who is the
Count de Roquefort?" It occasioned me no
surprise to hear from him only two days after
(his letter having crossed mine on the way),
that the fact of Roque's identity with the culprit was fully confirmed. And De Courcy
added: "It is not a suicide now, but, I fear, the
guillotine. How frightful! Who could believe it of the man we saw rioting among the
nymphs of Watteau?"

IV

I RETURNED to Paris by the way of Belgium.
I think it was in the Hôtel de Saxe, of Brus-
sels, where I first happened upon a budget of
French papers which contained a report of the
trial of poor Roque. It was a hopeless case

with him; every one foresaw that. For a time I do not think there was any sympathy felt for him. The testimony all went to show the harmless and benevolent character of the murdered Count. The culprit had appeared to all who saw him within the year past, of a morose and harsh disposition.

I say that for a time sympathy was with the murdered man; but certain circumstances came to light toward the close of the trial, and indeed after it was over, and the poor fellow's fate was fixed, which gave a new turn to popular feeling.

These circumstances had a special interest for me, inasmuch as they cleared up the mystery which had belonged to his change of manner in the galleries of the Louvre, and to his relations with the Count de Roquefort.

I will try and state these circumstances as they came to my knowledge through the newspaper reports of that date.

In the first place, the Count, after the visit of Emile Roque, had communicated to those in his confidence nothing respecting the nature or the objects of that visit; and this, notwithstanding he had such reason to apprehend violence on its repetition, that he had secured the presence of two officers to arrest the offensive

person. To these officers he had simply communicated the fact of his expecting a visit
from an *unknown* individual, who had threatened him with personal violence.

The officers were quite sure that the Count
had spoken of the criminal as a stranger to
him; indeed, he seemed eager to convey to
them the idea that he had no previous knowledge whatever of the individual who so cause-
lessly threatened his peace.

Nothing was found among the Count's papers to forbid the truthfulness of his assertion
on this point; no letter could be discovered
from any person bearing that name.

The mother of the prisoner, upon learning
the accusation urged against him, had become
incapacitated by a severe paralytic attack, from
appearing as a witness, or from giving any
intelligible information whatever. She had
said only, in the paroxysm of her distress, and
before her faculties were withered by the
shock: *"Lui aussi! Il s'y perd!"*

Not one of the companions of Emile Roque
(and he had many in his jovial days) had ever
heard him speak of the Count de Roquefort.
Up to the time of his departure for the South,
he had communicated to no one his intentions,
or even his destination. His old friends had,

indeed, remarked the late change in his manner, and had attributed it solely to what they supposed a bitter disappointment in relation to his proposed marriage with Virginie C——.

I have already alluded (through a letter from De Courcy) to the singular fact, that Emile Roque continued his familiarity and intimacy with Monsieur C—— long after the date of the change in his appearance, and even up to the time of his departure for the South. It was naturally supposed that Monsieur C—— would prove an important witness in the case. His testimony, however, so far from throwing light upon the crime, only doubled the mystery attaching to the prisoner's fate.

He spoke in the highest terms of the character which the criminal had always sustained. He confirmed the rumors which had coupled his name with that of a member of his own family. The marriage between the parties had been determined upon with his full consent, and only waited the final legal forms usual in such cases for its accomplishment, when it was deferred in obedience to the wishes of only M. Roque himself!

The witness regarded this as a caprice at the first; but the sudden change in the manner of the criminal from that time, had satisfied him that some secret anxiety was weighing on his mind. His high regard for the character of M. Roque prompted (and that alone had prompted) a continuance of intimacy with him, and a vain repetition of endeavors to win from him some explanation of his changed manner.

One fact more, which seemed to have special significance in its bearing upon the crime, was this:—in the pocket of the prisoner at the time of his seizure was found a letter purporting to be from the murdered Count, and addressed to a certain *Amedée Brune*. It was a tender letter, full of expressions of devotion, and promising that upon a day not very far distant, the writer would meet his fair one, and they should be joined together, for woe or for weal, thenceforth, through life. The letter was of an old date—thirty odd years ago it had been written; and on comparison with the manuscript of the Count of that date, gave evidence of authenticity. Who this Amedée Brune might be, or what relation she bore to the criminal, or how the letter came into his possession, none could tell. Those who had been early acquaintances of the Count had never so much as heard a mention of that name. A few went so far as to doubt the genuineness of his signature. He had been a man remarkable for his quiet and studious habits. So far as the knowledge of his friends extended, no passing gallantries had ever relieved the monotony of his life.

The accused, in the progress of the inquiries which had elicited these facts, had maintained a dogged silence, not communicating any statement of importance even to his legal advisers. The sudden illness which had befallen his mother, and which threatened a fatal termination, seemed to have done more to prostrate his hope and courage than the weight of the criminal accusation.

The *fiancée*, meantime, Mademoiselle C——, was, it seems, least of all interested in the fate of the prisoner. Whether incensed by his change of manner, or stung by jealousy, it was certain that before this accusation had been urged she had conceived against him a strong antipathy.

Such was the state of facts developed on the trial. The jury found him guilty of murder; there were no extenuating circumstances, and there was no recommendation to mercy.

After the condemnation the criminal had grown more communicative. Something of the reckless gayety of his old days had returned for a time. He amused himself with sketching from memory some of the heads of Watteau's nymphs upon his prison walls. His mother had died, fortunately, only a few days after the rendering of the verdict, without knowing, however, what fate was to befall her son.

It was rumored that when this event was made known to him he gave way to passionate tears, and sending for the priest, made a full confession of his crime and its causes. This confession had occasioned that turn in popular sympathy of which I have spoken. The friends of the Count, however, and even the prisoner's own legal advisers (as I was told), regarded it as only an ingenious appeal for mercy.

For myself, notwithstanding the lack of positive evidence to sustain his statements, I have been always inclined to believe his story a true one.

The main points in his confession were these: He had loved Virginie C——, as she had not deserved to be loved. He was happy; he had fortune, health, everything to insure content. Monsieur C—— welcomed him to his family. His mother rejoiced in the cheerfulness and sunny prospects of her only child. His father (he knew it only from his mother's lips) had been a general in the wars of Napoleon, and had died before his recollection.

He had been little concerned to inquire regarding the character or standing of his father, until, as the marriage day approached, it became necessary to secure legal testimonials respecting his patrimony and name.

No general by the name of Roque had ever served in the wars of Napoleon or in the armies of France! For the first time the laughing dream of his life was disturbed. With his heart full, and his brain on fire, he appealed to his mother for explanation. She had none to give. Amidst tears and sobs, the truth was wrung from her, that he—the gay-hearted Emile, whose life was full of promise—could claim no legal parentage. But the man who had so wronged both him and herself was still alive; and, with the weakness of her sex, she assured him that he was of noble birth, and had never shown tenderness toward any woman save herself.

Who was this noble father, on whose riches the son was living? No entreaties or threats could win this secret from the mother.

Then it was that the change had come over the character of Emile; then it was that he had deserted the smiling nymphs of Watteau for the despairing castaway of Géricault. Too proud to bring a tarnished escutcheon to his marriage rites; doubting if that stain would not cause both father and daughter to relent, he had himself urged the postponement of the legal arrangements. One slight hope—slighter than that belonging to the castaway of the wrecked *Méduse* —sustained him. The mother (she avowed it with tears and with grief) had become such only under solemn promise of marriage from one she had never doubted.

To find this recreant father was now the aim of the crazed life of Emile. With this frail hope electrifying his despair, he pushed his inquiries secretly in every quarter, and solaced his thought with his impassioned work in the corner salon of the Louvre.

In the chamber of his mother was a little *escritoire*, kept always closed and locked. His suspicions, after a time, attached themselves there. He broke the fastenings, and found within a miniature, a lock of hair, a packet of letters, signed—De Roquefort. Of these last he kept only one; the others he destroyed as so many tokens of his shame.

That fatal one he bore with him away from Paris, out from the influence of his mother. He pushed his inquiries with the insidious cunning of a man crazed by a single thought. He found at length the real address of the Count de Roquefort. He hurried to his presence, bearing always with him the letter of promise, so ruthlessly broken.

The Count was startled by his appearance, and startled still more by the wildness of his story and of his demands. The son asked the father to make good, at this late day, the promise of his youth. The Count replied evasively; he promised to assist the claimant with money, and with his influence, and would engage to make him heir to the larger part of his fortune. All this fell coldly upon the ear of the excited Emile. He wished restitution to his mother. Nothing less could be listened to.

The Count urged the scandal which would grow out of such a measure; with his years and reputation, he could not think of exposing himself to the ribald tongues of the world. Moreover, the publicity which must necessarily belong to the marriage would, he considered, be of serious injury to Emile himself. The fact of his illegitimacy was unknown; the old relation of his mother to himself was a secret one; the obstacles which might now lie in the way of his own marriage to Virginie C—— were hardly worth consideration, when compared with the inconvenience which would follow a public exposure of the circumstances. He set before Emile the immense advantages of the fortune which he would secure to him on his (the Count's) death, provided only he was content to forbear his urgence as regarded his mother.

Emile listened coldly, calmly. There was but one thought in his mind—only one hope; there must be restitution to his mother, or he would take justice in his own hands. The Count must make good his promise, or the consequences would be fatal. He gave the Count two days for reflection.

At the end of that time he returned, prepared for any emergency. The Count had utterly refused him justice: he had uttered his own death-warrant.

His mother was no longer living, to feel the sting of the exposure. For himself, he had done all in his power to make her name good: he had no ties to the world; he was ready for the worst.

Such was the relation of Emile; and there was a coherency about it, and an agreement with the main facts established by evidence, which gave it an air of great probability.

But, on the other hand, it was alleged by the friends of the Count that such a relation on his part never could have existed; that not the slightest evidence of it could be found among his papers, nor did the recollection of his oldest friends offer the smallest confirmation. The reported conversations of Emile with the Count were, they contended, only an ingenious fiction.

Singularly enough, there was nothing among the effects of the deceased Madame Roque to confirm the allegation that she had ever borne the name of Amedée Brune. She had been known only to her oldest acquaintances of the capital as Madame Roque: of her previous history nothing could be ascertained.

The solitary exclamation of that lady, "*Il s'y perd!*" was instanced as proof that Emile was laboring under a grievous delusion.

Notwithstanding this, my own impression was that Emile had executed savage justice upon the betrayer of his mother.

V

ON the month of March—a very cold month in that year—I had returned to Paris, and taken up my old quarters in a *hôtel garni* of the Rue des Beaux-Arts.

Any public interest or curiosity which had belonged to the trial and story of Emile Roque had passed away. French journalists do not

keep alive an interest of that sort by any reports upon the condition of the prisoner. They
barely announce the execution of his sentence
upon the succeeding day. I had, by accident
only, heard of his occasional occupation in
sketching the heads of some of Watteau's
nymphs upon the walls of his cell. I could
scarce believe this of him. It seemed to me
that his fancy would run rather in the direction
of the horrors of Géricault.

I felt an irresistible desire to see him once
again. There was no hope of this, except I
should be present at his execution. I had never
witnessed an execution; had never cared to
witness one. But I wished to look once more
on the face of Emile Roque.

The executions in Paris take place without
public announcement, and usually at daybreak,
upon the square fronting the great prison of
La Roquette. No order is issued until a late
hour on the preceding evening, when the state
executioner is directed to have the guillotine
brought at midnight to the prison square, and
a corps of soldiery is detailed for *special* service (unmentioned) in that quarter of the city.
My only chance of witnessing the scene was in
arranging with one of the small wine-mer-
chants, who keep open house in that neigh-

borhood until after midnight, to dispatch a messenger to me whenever he should see preparations commenced.

This arrangement I effected; and on the 22d of March I was roused from sleep at a little before one in the morning by a bearded man, who had felt his way up the long flight of stairs to my rooms, and informed me that the guillotine had arrived before the prison of Roquette.

My thought flashed on the instant to the figure of Emile as I had seen him before the shepherdesses of Watteau—as I had seen him before the picture of the Shipwreck. I dressed hurriedly, and groped my way below. The night was dark and excessively cold. A little sleet had fallen, which crumpled under my feet as I made my way toward the quay. Arrived there, not a cab was to be found at the usual stand; so I pushed on across the river, and under the archway of the palace of the Louvre, —casting my eye toward that wing of the great building where I had first seen the face which I was shortly to look on for the last time on earth.

Finding no cabs in the square before the palace, I went on through the dark streets of St. Anne and Grammont, until I reached the

Boulevard. A few *voitures de remise* were opposite the Café Foy. I appealed to the drivers of two of them in vain, and only succeeded by a bribe in inducing a third to drive me to the *Place de la Roquette*. It is a long way from the centre of Paris, under the shadow almost of *Père la Chaise*. I tried to keep some reckoning of the streets through which we passed, but I could not. Sometimes my eye fell upon what seemed a familiar corner, but in a moment all was strange again. The lamps appeared to me to burn dimly; the houses along the way grew smaller and smaller. From time to time, I saw a wine-shop still open; but not a soul was moving on the streets with the exception of, here and there, a brace of *sergents de ville*. At length we seemed to have passed out of the range even of the city patrol, and I was beginning to entertain very unpleasant suspicions of the cabman, and of the quarter into which he might be taking me at that dismal hour of the night, when he drew up his horse before a little wine-shop, which I soon recognized as the one where I had left my order for the dispatch of the night's messenger.

I knew now that the guillotine was near.

As I alighted I could see, away to my right,

the dim outline of the prison looming against the night sky, with not a single light in its gratings. The broad square before it was sheeted over with sleet, and the leafless trees that girdled it round stood ghost-like in the snow. Through the branches, and not far from the prison gates, I could see, in the gray light (for it was now hard upon three o'clock), a knot of persons collected around a frame-work of timber, which I knew must be the guillotine.

I made my way there, the frozen surface crumpling under my steps. The workmen had just finished their arrangements. Two of the city police were there, to preserve order, and to prevent too near an approach of the loiterers from the wine-shops—who may have been, perhaps, at this hour, a dozen in number.

I could pass near enough to observe fully the construction of the machine. There was, first, a broad platform, perhaps fifteen feet square, supported by movable tressle-work, and elevated some six or seven feet from the ground. A flight of plank steps led up to this, broad enough for three to walk upon abreast. Immediately before the centre of these steps, upon the platform, was stretched what seemed a trough of plank; and from the farther end of this trough rose two strong uprights of timber, perhaps ten feet in height. These were connected at the top by a slight frame-work; and immediately below this, by the light of a solitary street lamp which flickered near by, I could see the glistening of the knife. Beside the trough-like box was placed a long willow basket: its shape explained to me its purpose. At the end of the trough, and beyond the upright timbers, was placed a tub: with a shudder, I recognized its purpose also.

The prison gates were only a few rods distant from the steps to the scaffold and directly opposite them. They were still closed and dark.

The execution, I learned, was to take place at six. A few loiterers, mostly in blouses, came up from time to time to join the group about the scaffold.

By four o'clock there was the sound of tramping feet, one or two quick words of command, and presently a battalion of the Municipal Guard, without drum-beat, marched in at the lower extremity of the square, approached the scaffold, and having stacked their arms, loitered with the rest.

Lights now began to appear at the windows of the prison. A new corps of police came up and cleared a wider space around the guillotine. A cold gray light stole slowly over the eastern sky.

By five o'clock the battalion of the Guards had formed a hedge of bayonets from either side of the prison doors, extending beyond and inclosing the scaffold. A squadron of mounted men had also come upon the ground, and was drawn up in line, a short distance on one side. Two officials appeared now upon the scaffold, and gave trial to the knife. They let slip the cord or chain which held it to its place, and the knife fell with a quick, sharp clang, that I thought must have reached to ears within the walls of the prison. Twice more they made their trial, and twice more I heard the clang.

Meantime people were gathering. Market-women bound for the city lingered at sight of the unusual spectacle, and a hundred or more soldiers from a neighboring barrack had now joined the crowd of lookers-on. A few women from the near houses had brought their children; and a half-dozen boys had climbed into the trees for a better view.

At intervals, from the position which I held, I could see the prison doors open for a moment, and the light of a lantern within, as some officer passed in or out.

I remember that I stamped the ground petulantly—it was so cold. Again and again I looked at my watch.

Fifteen minutes to six!

It was fairly daylight now, though the morning was dark and cloudy, and a fine, searching mist was in the air.

A man in blouse placed a bag of saw-dust at the foot of the gallows. The crowd must have now numbered a thousand. An old market-woman stood next me. She saw me look at my watch, and asked the hour.

"Eight minutes to six."

"*Mon Dieu; huit minutes encore!*" She was eager for the end.

I could have counted time now by the beating of my heart.

What was Emile Roque doing within those doors? praying? struggling? was the face of the castaway on him? I could not separate him now from that fearful picture; I was straining my vision to catch a glimpse—not of Emile Roque—but of the living counterpart of that terrible expression which he had wrought—wild, aimless despair.

Two minutes of six.

I saw a hasty rush of men to the parapet that topped the prison wall; they leaned there, looking over.

EMILE ROQUE

I saw a stir about the prison gates, and both were flung wide open.

There was a suppressed murmur around me —"*Le voici! Le voici!*" I saw him coming forward between two officers; he wore no coat or waistcoat, and his shirt was rolled back from his throat; his arms were pinioned behind him; his bared neck was exposed to the frosty March air; his face was pale—deathly pale, yet it was calm; I recognized not the castaway, but the man—Emile Roque.

There was a moment between the prison gates and the foot of the scaffold; he kissed the crucifix, which a priest handed him, and mounted with a firm step. I know not how, but in an instant he seemed to fall, his head toward the knife—under the knife.

My eyes fell. I heard the old woman beside me say passionately, "*Mon Dieu! il ne veut pas!*"

I looked toward the scaffold; at that supreme moment the brute instinct in him had rallied for a last struggle. Pinioned as he was, he had lifted up his brawny shoulders and withdrawn his neck from the fatal opening. Now indeed, his face wore the terrible expression of the picture. Hate, fear, madness, despair, were blended in his look.

But the men mastered him; they thrust him down; I could see him writhe vainly. My eyes fell again.

I heard a clang—a thud!

There was a movement in the throng around me. When I looked next at the scaffold, a man in blouse was sprinkling saw-dust here and there. Two others were lifting the long willow basket into a covered cart. I could see now that the guillotine was painted of a dull red color, so that no blood stains would show.

I moved away with the throng, the sleet crumpling under my feet.

I could eat nothing that day. I could not sleep on the following night.

The bloodshot eyes and haggard look of the picture which had at the last—as I felt it would be—been made real in the man, haunted me.

I never go now to the gallery of the Louvre but I shun the painting of the wrecked Medusa as I would shun a pestilence.

THE ATTIC

UNDER THE ROOF

THE ATTIC

UNDER THE ROOF

I CANNOT but think it very odd—the distinctness with which I remember the little speech which the head-master of our school made to "us boys," on a November morning—just after prayer-time—twenty-odd years ago! He gave an authoritative rap with the end of his ruler upon the desk—glared about the room a moment, through his spectacles,—as if to awe us into a due attitude of attention, and then spoke in this wise:— "Those boys who sleep in the attic—(a long pause here,) should understand that they are expected to conduct themselves like gentlemen, and set a proper example to the rest of the school. (I think he singled out Judkins and Barton here, with a sharp look over the rim of his glasses.) Last night I am very sorry to say there was great disorder. Several large field-pumpkins (a very perceptible titter here along the benches, which the head-master represses by a 'rat-tat-tat' from the ruler)—

several large field-pumpkins were rolled through the corridor at a late hour of the night, and finally were tumbled down the attic stairs—disturbing the sleep of the quiet boys, and alarming the household. I hope the conduct will not be repeated."

As I had not at that day been promoted to the attic, but classed myself with the quiet ones whose sleep had been disturbed, I listened with a good deal of modest coolness to this speech: indeed the master, as he stepped down from the platform, patted me approvingly on the head (I being conveniently posted to receive that mark of regard), and I could not but reproach myself thereupon, for the glee with which I, in company with a few others who were in the secret, had listened for the bowling pumpkins as they came bounding down the stairs the night before.

The real culprits of the attic, however, were Judkins, Barton and Russel; and I looked upon these ringleaders, I remember, with a good deal of awe—wondering if their misdeeds and great daring would not some day bring them to the penitentiary.

I am happy to say, however, that they have thus far escaped: One of them, Russel, is indeed an active politician; but the others are quite safe. Judkins, who leered in such a way that morning at his chum,—as I thought the very height of youthful address and villainy, is now the stout rector of a flourishing church somewhere in one of the Middle States; and wears, I am told, the most dignified figure— in his gown—of any clergyman of his Diocese.

Barton I had neither seen nor heard of in many years. He was of British parentage, and there was a rumor that at his father's death, which occurred shortly after those school-days to which I have referred, he had gone back with his mother, to the old country. Whether the rumor was well founded or not, I probably never should have been informed, had it not been for certain incidents hinted at under mention of "my old school-mate of the Attic," in the little fat English note-book spoken of in the opening chapters, and which is just now lying under my hand. I will try to group those incidents together carefully enough to make a half-story—if nothing more.

I was bowling down through Devonshire upon a coach top—it was before the time of the South Devon rail-way—somewhere between Exeter and Totness, when my attention was arrested by a rubicund-faced man sitting behind me, and who wore a communicativeness of look, which anywhere in England, it is quite refreshing and startling to behold. I fell speedily into conversation with him, and at almost every word detected traces of a voice I had some day listened to before; they were traces of the old boy of the attic. An allusion or two to other-side matters—most of all the naming of the little village where the great school crowned the hill—opened his memory like a book. It was Barton himself. Having been one of the junior boys, my own face was not so familiar to him; for a pretty long period in life we study only the faces before us; but when members of the younger ranks begin to crowd us, we look back with some scrutiny to find what manner of men they are.

Howbeit we fell now into most easy and familiar chat; we went back to the days of "taw" and roundabouts as easily as a cloud drifts. I think our companions of the coach top must have been immensely mystified by our talk about the "Principal" and his daughters and his sons—one of whom was the pattern of all mischief. How we roared that day as we compared recollections about the plethoric, thickset, irascible farmer whose orchard lay unfortunately contiguous to the play-ground! How we probed the mysteries of the smoky, reeking kitchen and brought up to light the old *chef de cuisine* (poor woman, she is dead this many a day) with her top-knot curls and her flying cap-strings! And I am persuaded that those "field-pumpkins" rumbling down the attic stairs, did not give more innocent merriment to any listener on the eventful night, than to us old boys—that day in Devon. Of course we had our little observations to make about our old friend Judkins and his rectorship; and if they were not altogether such as his lady admirers of the parish (of whom I am told he has a warm galaxy) might commend,—they were at least honest and cheery, and respectful to the man, and still more respectful, I trust, to the great cause in which he is a worker.

Afterward, as our hilarity subsided somewhat, we fell into talk about our own personal history—a subject which, so far as I have observed, is apt to command, whenever approached, a certain degree of seriousness. It is all very well to be merry at the recollection of some old school-mate, who has recklessly married and gone astray,—or of one who is putting all his thews and muscle to the strain of a contest with some great giant of worldly trouble (it mattering very little whether the giant is imaginary or real)—or of another, floating about in weary idleness and bachelorhood, seeming very chirruppy on the surface— a surface which is apt to gloss over a great many tormenting fires. This sort of observation, as I said, we can conduct with a certain degree of cheery warmth and abandon;—it concerns our neighbors' gold fields, not ours; —but when we come to compare notes about the value of our own working veins, and to confess the small weight and richness of ore we have brought up after all our digging,— it breeds a seriousness. We smile at thought of the rector in connection with his boyish wildness; but have we any rectorship—any parish that looks to us for guidance? We crack our little jokes at mention of poor Tom Steady fighting wearily his long battle with the world with wife and children tugging at his skirts;—have we any such battle to fight? or if we had, should we fight it as patiently as he?

There was not very much to interest in my part of the discourse, into which the current of our chat fell, there upon the Devon coach —since up to that date, I had been living only a drifting life of invalid vagabondage. The rubicund face of Barton told a different story.

He was, if I remember rightly, concerned in some manufacturing interest near to the old town of Modbury; he had a pleasant cottage thereabout among the hills, to which he gave me a very cordial invitation.

I rejoiced in his pleasant establishment: he must be married—of course?

"Yes ——," he says, with some coyness— "married;" and he continues in a lowered tone, and with an embarrassment, I thought, in his manner—"there are some inconvenient circumstances however:—to tell you the truth, my wife is not living with me at present; so if you drive over, I can give you only a bachelor welcome."

"Ah!" (What could I say more?)

There is a pause for a while in our talk. At length Barton breaks in:—

"Looks awkwardly, I de'say?"

"Well—it does."

"It *is* awkward," said he, with some feeling; "it worries me excessively."

"I'm not surprised," I ventured to say; but farther than this I made no observation. If there is one bit of counsel which is absolutely sound, both for friends and strangers, it is— never to meddle with quarrels between husband and wife; domestic troubles are a great deal more apt to cure themselves than they are to be cured by outsiders. I was not sorry to find that, by the time the conversation had reached this critical stage, the coach had drawn up by the inn-door, near to the market-cross of the old town of Totness, to which place I had booked myself. I shook hands with my newly-found acquaintance, promising to pay him an early visit.

It was quite certain that he was not growing thin under the "worry;" I think I never met with a better candidate for acceptance by the Life Insurance people. Presentable withal; not over six and thirty at the outside; amiable in his expression—though this to be sure is a very doubtful indication of character. Possibly the wife was a victim to the entertainment of jealous fancies; for I could not but admit, that there was a good deal of the air of a "gallant, gay Lothario," about my friend Barton.

I think I must have passed a fortnight or three weeks at a little village in the neighborhood—strolling up and down the hillsides that are kept constantly begreened by a thousand irrigating streamlets,—indulging in an occasional idle canter along the country roads, and once, at least, whipping a lazy meadow-stretch of the Erme river with tackle I had borrowed at the inn; and long ago as the visit was made, I think I could find my way now to a certain pool, not far below the Erme-bridge on the Modbury road, and within sight of Fleetwood House, where upon a good day, and with a good wind at one's back, I think an adroit fly-fisher might be very sure of a pound "strike."

But even such pleasant employment did not drive wholly out of mind Barton, his solitary home at Clumber Cottage, and my promised visit. So I named a day to him by post, and received a warm reply—setting forth however his request that I would make "no allusion to the unpleasant circumstance mentioned in the coach-drive—more particularly as he was rated by all the members of his present establishment, and by the neighborhood, only as a gay bachelor. Bating this little awkwardness," he continued, in this note, "I shall hope to give you a *fricassée* that will equal that of the old *chef de cuisine* under whose presiding curls and cap we broke bread together last."

I drove down in a jaunty dog-cart with which they equipped me at the inn. Clumber Cottage was neither a large nor a pretentious establishment; there was a tidy array of gravel walks; great piles of luxuriant rhododendron and Spanish laurel; a gray stone cottage with its flanking stable, half hidden in a copse of evergreens; cosey rooms with a large flow of sunshine into their southern windows; a perfect snuggery in short, where I found as hospitable welcome as it was possible for a single man to give.

I shall not dwell upon the strolls and upon the talk we indulged in on that mild February day. The course of neither threw any new light upon the matter which had so piqued my curiosity. A snug and quiet dinner with its salmon, its haunch of exquisite Dartmoor mutton, its ruby glow of sherry in the master's cups, and its fragrant bouquet of Latour chased away the early hours of evening. A tidy waiting maid attended us, whose face, I am free to confess—after a good deal of not incurious observation,—was of a degree of plainness which must have proved satisfactory to the most capricious and despotic of wives.

I bade, as I supposed, a final adieu to my host next morning, and set off on my return to Totness, and thence to Exeter. Barton had undoubtedly made a terribly false step—not of a character to be talked of; and though I pitied him sincerely, I could not help thinking that he wore his disappointment with extraordinary resolution and appetite.

The cold fogs of Exeter, a cough, and the advice of a friendly physician, drove me back again to one of those little bights along the Channel shore where the sun makes an almost Mediterranean mildness even in winter. Ten days after my dinner with Barton, I found myself established in two delightful rooms just under the roof of a lodging house in Torquay. Vines clambered over the windows, and shook their tresses of rich ivy leaves on either side, as I looked out upon the bay, which lay below—fair, and clear and smooth, with a score or more of fishing boats lying drawn up on the lip of the sands by Paignton, and beyond. This cosey wintering place for delicate people, is in fact so nestled into the flank of a protecting circuit of hills, that on all the little terraces where cottages find lodgment, you may see lemon trees and the oleander blooming out of doors in winter. A harsh storm may indeed compel special and temporary protection; but a sunny day and a south-east wind bring such budding spring again as can be found nowhere else in England.

In such a place, of course, every lodging house has its little company—not necessarily known to each other, but meeting day after day in the entrance hall, or in the pretty green yard, set off with flowers and shrubbery, which lies before the entrance door.

Upon the same floor with myself was another single lodger who was thoroughly English, I think, in all that regarded his moral qualities; but physically, a very poor type—inasmuch as he was a weazen, dyspeptic, dried man, who wore yellow gaiters, a spotted cravat, and a huge eye-glass dangling at the top button hole of his waistcoat. His calls upon the waiting maid, Mary, were most inordinate and irrepressible—sometimes for hot water, sometimes for cold—the hot water being always too hot, and the cold not cold enough; I think he would have driven the poor girl mad with his fretfulness, if he had not anointed her palm from week to week with a crown or two of service money. I sometimes took my coffee at an adjoining table in the little breakfast room upon the ground floor; but after a series of resolute approaches I never came nearer to acquaintanceship than passing a "Good morning" to him; and even this he met invariably with so captious and churlish a rejoinder, that for very sport's sake, I kept up the show of civility to the last morning of my stay. I have no doubt that he entertained a certain respect for the Church of England and the prayer book; but I am sure that he would have thought very contemptuously of Death or of any prospective Heaven or Hell, which were not occasionally spoken encouragingly of by the Times Newspaper.

Upon the second floor was an elderly invalid lady, whom I frequently saw seated, in sunny weather, at her open window, or in her easy chair upon the grass plat below. She was attended by her maid and by her daughter; this last a fair young girl, of most lithe and graceful figure, and with one of those winning faces which a man never grows tired of looking on. I think I see her now hovering about her mother's chair, offering a hundred little attentions —now beating the pillows, that the position may be made the easier,—now pleading with her to taste some new delicacy,—now seated beside her, with one of those drooping willowy flats half hiding her face, as she reads for the ear of the invalid some fragment from a favorite book or journal. Both mother and daughter wore the deepest black, and the widow's cap told only too plainly the cause of their mourning.

Upon the same floor with these last, and making up the tale of our lodgers, was a young mother, the wife of an officer of the

Indian civil service, who had brought down to this balmy atmosphere a sick child; every day the poor little fellow, with a languid expression that promised I thought small hope, was rolled down in a Bath-chair to a sunny position on the shore of the bay; every day the hopeful mother walked anxiously beside him, looking for a returning strength—which never came.

With explorations about the charming nooks of the little town of Torquay, and with not a little furtive observation of the personages I have enumerated, and to all of whom my quality of lodger permitted me to give passing salutations from day to day, I passed a fortnight. In the course of that time I had learned incidentally that the lady and daughter who had attracted a large share of my observation, were the widow and child of a Colonel Wroxley who had been killed or reported missing, in the India service (I think it was about the time of the Afghan war). The blow, wholly unexpected, had almost crushed the wife, who was previously in delicate health, and who had now come with her only child to struggle under that balmy atmosphere against her misfortune. Upon her first arrival, I was told, she had frequently enjoyed the promenade along the sands; but to the great grief of the daughter, she had now given up these little excursions, and relapsed into a state of despondency and listlessness which grew every day more decided. The daughter at the instigation of both mother and physician tore herself away for an hour each evening for a stroll along the beach, sometimes alone, and sometimes attended by a young acquaintance from a neighboring cottage.

Now it happened one day, toward the end of my first fortnight of stay,—as I was returning from my usual afternoon tramp,—that I caught sight before me in the dusk, of this fair young girl—who had so enlisted my admiration and sympathy—accompanied by a gentleman whose bearing toward her, and whose familiarity, should have been that only of an accepted lover. I quickened my pace as they drew near the gateway to catch a fuller sight of this stranger. As I did so, they suddenly turned to double upon their walk again; and I cannot tell what horror and disgust came over me when I saw that her attendant was none other than Barton! He knew me at once, but met me with a surprised and embarrassed manner; and I dare say that my own was equally embarrassed, and I am quite sure, not very cordial. He expressed his wonder at finding me still in Devon, asked my address, and passed on.

I had however no call from him the next day, or on any subsequent day. Miss Wroxley met my salutation next morning with a deep blush; but I saw in her the same loving, gentle, unwearied care for her invalid mother. That so lovely a creature should become the victim of a scoundrel was a thing too terrible to think of.

It was plain now—the cause of his domestic infelicity; the man must be a roué of the worst description. I could think only with disgust and abhorrence of my intercourse with him, and of my day's visit at Clumber Cottage. I found myself reckoning up, as nearly as I could, his old habitudes and tendencies at school; and it seemed to me plainly enough that they all had a leaning toward the worst forms of baseness. I even thought of making a confidant of the weazen-faced gentleman; but when I saw him shuffling into the breakfast room with his pinched hungry look, and heard his captious "Good morning," and saw him thrust his glass into the socket of his eye for a new gloat over some prowess of "my Lord Aberdeen" or of "my Lord Darby"—I relented.

Matters remained in this state—I seeing no more of Barton—when one morning I became conscious of an excitement pervading the whole household. The eyes of the maid fairly twinkled; "boots" even was full of glee; the poor mother, whose child was near death, wore an expression of tranquil pleasure, in her anxiety; but, most of all, the change showed itself in Miss Wroxley, whose face as I caught sight of it from the window, was fairly radiant.

It was explained to me when I went below: news had come that Colonel Wroxley, the father, was not killed, but had escaped just now from a long captivity, and was safely on his way for England. The wife only, did not share in the joy; her hopes had been too deeply shattered; a hint alone of the possible truth had been conveyed to her by her daughter; but even this had been repulsed with a shudder of disbelief, and an entreaty that she might hear no more of such rumors, which had appalled the poor girl. The physician upon his morning visit had declared that the communication of such news, if urged upon her acceptance, in her present state of health, might give a shock that would be fatal.

Meantime the husband is approaching England; the poor lady does not rally; a dozen different plans are devised to prepare her for the strange revulsion of feeling; but they all fail of accomplishment; at the least approach to the forbidden topic, she refuses, in a tempest of despair, all hearing.

Barton I have not met again; but on one or two occasions, when Miss Wroxley has returned after dusk, I have observed her lingering at the wicket, and have heard a male voice at the parting. Once or twice too, my eye has fallen upon a letter in the post-man's budget for "Miss Wroxley"—written in a hand I know only too well. There can be no doubt that he is making his way insidiously—indeed has made it already, into the full affections of this sweet girl. It can be no affair of cousinship; else, why this avoidance of the mother and of the house? why the avoidance of me?

Upon a certain morning somewhat later, the house is stirred again by the intelligence that the little fevered boy is dead. The mother's grief is violent and explosive. The poor wan creature who has lingered so long doubtfully between night and day, is at length placidly stretched in sleep. Yet the mother cannot abide the change from fevered pain to eternal quietude. Her noisy grief stirs the heart of her invalid neighbor. At last—at last, there is a heart that mourns, as she has mourned.

The quick sympathy tells upon every fibre of her being. She must join tears with this bereaved one. She insists upon going to her; she finds a strength she has not found this many a day. It is even so; we are tied to life, and find capacity for endurance, more in companionship of grief, than in any companionship of joy.

The physician shrewdly perceives that advantage should be taken of this exaltation of feeling for communicating news of the speedy return of the husband. The willing daughter receives the needed instructions. She bounds toward her one day as the mother returns from her errand of mercy—throws herself in her arms—"It is true, mamma, it *is* true: He is alive and we shall see him again!"

"My poor child—what do you tell me?"

"True—true, mother: he is alive, he is on his way: there is a letter in his own hand that tells us."

And the woman bows her head over her child—"My God, I thank thee!"

"No faltering now, mother; your poor friend with her dead boy by her, needs all your strength—all your repose to cheer her. Don't desert her."

A little rally—a deadly nervous tremor—

one wild gush of tears, and the conquest is made.

"And now the letter, my darling,—the letter —quick, give me the letter; these old eyes must spell it out."

Can it be that a new and deadlier grief hangs threatening over this family—that courage and strength come so suddenly, for the strain?

I had the pleasure of witnessing the arrival of Col. Wroxley before my leave of that delightful town of Torquay. A tall swarthy man, bronzed by those fierce suns of India, firmly knit in muscle and in temper—a man whose will I thought would be an iron one, but whose heart under it—though making little demonstration—might sometimes melt like iron in a furnace; a man to be trusted—not lightly provoked—above all, a man to be obeyed.

It seemed to me that such a protector—perhaps avenger—might some day be needed.

The little boy is buried; we had all followed him to his last sleeping place upon a sunny spot of the hill-side; the mother is taking on a calm courage; the widow's caps are abandoned, and I see the figure of the colonel's daughter flitting under the trees, of a mild evening, clad all in white. A sober cheerfulness is growing upon all the household—with one marked exception. The daughter, at the first so radiant with joy at the father's return, is wearing day by day a more disturbed look. There is a fitfulness in her manner which has not belonged to her. I see her less often with her young companions. And I am somehow conscious of the presence of some party hovering about the shades of the hill-road at evening —eager to snatch a word—to multiply promises—to fasten a deeper hold upon her affections.

It is plain that the father sees this altered condition of his daughter's feeling, and in his awkward, soldierly way, endeavors to brighten her spirits. And he enters upon the task with all the more eagerness, since he has already in days past laid his iron rule against what he had judged her caprices. But the story of his own wife's immeasurable grief has opened his eyes to the depth and breadth of that law of the affections which no mere exercise of authoritative will, whether outside or within, can bound or measure. No man's affections— much less woman's—can be ordered "to the front." The autocrat of Russia, magnanimous as he is, in many of his designs, is wearying and bloodying himself against this rule of our nature, all over the Polish plains.

I have said that the colonel in other days had overruled the daughter's caprice. A certain young acquaintance of his and son of an old friend, who had been attracted—as who had not—by the graces of his daughter, the colonel had fixed upon with quite military resolve, as his future son-in-law. He had studied his character well; he was worthy; he was every inch a soldier; he would make his daughter happy; and Annie must look upon the matter as settled.

The mother had expostulated; but the soldier's fiery will, and her exalted sense of duty brought her to capitulation. The news of the colonel's death, instead of giving freedom to the child, had inspired the mother with an insensate wish to carry out to the last degree the wishes of the father. God had made her the legatee of the colonel's uncontrollable will.

But now this barrier to the parental confidence was removed. The young aide-de-camp had been killed in battle. What could mean then those tears—that fitfulness—that overcasting shadow of trouble? I felt that a catastrophe was approaching. And it came.

But the letter that announced it did not

reach me until I had left Torquay. I was at the Albemarle, London, when this exultant note was handed me—post-marked Modbury —from Barton:

"MY DEAR SIR,

"You must have thought I treated you very scurvily. Annie thought it best however that I should not call at your lodgings. We had been privately married a year before. Though I ought not to say it, the colonel's return to life was something of a damper to me; but he knows it all now, and is thoroughly reconciled. I can show him a rent-roll from my little ventures hereabout, that is larger than his colonel's pay. We are all at Clumber Cottage—happy of course.

"If you will run down to pass a day with us, I will give you something better than the old bachelor greeting.

"Truly y'rs."

I was not a little taken aback by this cheery letter. I began to reflect again upon the old school-boy qualities which I thought I had seen developed in him. They were not so bad after all.

I never hear a man rashly and wantonly abused—in fact, scarce ever read my morning paper—but I think with compunction of my sins in that direction, at my quiet lodgings *Under the Roof,* in the town of Torquay.

FINIAL

THUS far the memories suggested by my little note-books have carried me, until I have reached the last half-story, lying under the roof.

I put them back now upon their corner of the Library shelf—hoping they will have opened the way to the hearts of some new friends, and not rebuffed the kindly spirit of such old ones as I claimed years ago.

The little books shall have a long rest now: and whatever I venture upon in future, in an imaginative humor, shall have its seat nearer home. It is not so much in way of apology, or of promise, that I say this, as it is for the adjustment of some neat *finial* for the peak of the roof of my building of—SEVEN STORIES.

Lightning Source UK Ltd.
Milton Keynes UK
UKHW010707050119
334854UK00005B/807/P